FIRST-CLASS TROUBLEMAKER

Mr. Broderick called the class to attention and began the day's lesson. As the teacher was talking, a motion in the row next to Jana caught her eye. Geena McNatt was holding a ruler, and she was using it to slowly push the books on the corner of Mona Vaughn's desk off the edge.

Jana watched, frozen in her seat for a second. Should she warn Mona? Before she could decide what to do, the books went crashing to the floor.

Mona nearly jumped out of her chair, and Mr. Broderick stopped speaking as everyone turned to see what had happened.

Mona's face turned bright red. "Sorry," she said in a tiny voice.

Geena really is a menace, Jana thought angrily. First she took Whitney Larkin's homework, and now she's knocked Mona's books onto the floor. I don't mind her picking on me, but why does she have to pick on people like Mona and Whitney? *Something had to be done about Geena McNatt.*

THE FABULOUS FIVE

Seventh-Grade Menace

BETSY HAYNES

A BANTAM SKYLARK BOOK®
NEW YORK • TORONTO • LONDON • SYDNEY • AUCKLAND

RL 5, IL age 9 and up

SEVENTH-GRADE MENACE
A Bantam Skylark Book / December 1989

ISBN 0-553-15763-9

Published simultaneously in the United States and Canada

Bantam Books are published by Bantam Books, a division of Bantam Doubleday Dell Publishing Group, Inc. Its trademark, consisting of the words "Bantam Books" and the portrayal of a rooster, is Registered in U.S. Patent and Trademark Office and in other countries. Marca Registrada. Bantam Books, 666 Fifth Avenue, New York, New York 10103.

PRINTED IN THE UNITED STATES OF AMERICA

CW   0 9 8 7 6 5 4 3 2 1

To Susan Korman

CHAPTER

1

Jana Morgan flashed her biggest and brightest smile at Randy Kirwan as she crossed the Wakeman Junior High school grounds and headed toward The Fabulous Five's favorite spot by the fence. He waved and gave her his 1,000-watt smile back.

Even though it was Monday morning, Jana was still daydreaming about their super weekend together. On Friday night, they had gone to the movies and Bumpers, the fast-food restaurant where everyone from Wakeman Junior High hung out. On Saturday, Randy had bicycled to her house, and her stepfather Pink had dropped them off at the West Side Mall, where they'd met the rest of The Fabulous Five: Katie Shannon, Beth Barry, Melanie Edwards, and Christie Winchell, who were there with Tony Calcaterra, Keith Masterson, Shane Arrington, Scott Daly, and Jon Smith. Later, they had all gone to Melanie's to watch a video and eat popcorn. The evening had ended with Randy's holding her hand as he walked her home and kissing her good-night before getting on his bicycle and leaving. Jana knew she had a dopey smile on her face as she thought about the terrific weekend, but she didn't care. Let people stare.

"HEY, GET OUT OF THE WAY!"

Before Jana could react, someone slammed into her, knocking her backward. She tried to catch her balance, but she tripped instead. Her books flew in all directions as she hit the ground with a thud.

"Why don't you watch where you're going?"

Geena McNatt stood there, glaring down at Jana. She was dressed in a pair of red sweatpants and matching top, which were both several sizes too big for her. She had one hand on her hip and was holding a football with the other.

"I was walking where people are supposed to walk!" Jana retorted angrily. How in the world could Geena accuse her of being at fault? Jana got to her feet and faced the other girl.

Geena had reddish-brown hair that she hardly ever combed and freckles across the bridge of her nose. She was a year older and half a head taller than Jana, even though she was in the seventh grade, too. Jon Smith, who had gone to Copper Beach Elementary with Geena, had told Christie that Geena had been held back in the fifth grade.

Even though Jana and Geena were both in Mr. Broderick's social studies class, Jana hadn't talked to her very much. In fact, Jana tried to stay out of her way. Geena was always picking on kids who couldn't defend themselves and disrupting the classroom.

"Well, you'd better watch where you're walking," Geena said, turning to throw the football in a perfect spiral to Bill Soliday and trotting after it.

"Are you okay?" Randy asked, running up.

Jana brushed off the back of her denim skirt and checked the scrape on her elbow. "I think so. I didn't see her coming."

"I'm not surprised. She was running after a pass, and you were looking the other way."

As Randy started picking up Jana's books, the rest of The Fabulous Five joined them. They had been Jana's best friends for what seemed like forever, and she knew she could always count on them. Now they were all giving her sympathetic looks.

"I think they should outlaw throwing footballs on the school ground," said Beth. "It's dangerous."

"Only when Geena McNatt's playing," said Christie. "The guys are more careful than she is."

"I don't think I broke anything," said Jana. "It was just an accident."

"Are you sure you don't have footprints up your back?" asked Keith Masterson, who had just walked up. "Geena almost stepped on you."

Jana smiled. "I'm fine." And except for a few sore spots, she did feel fine. It had just been an accident, she told herself, and even though Geena was in her social studies class, she might not have to speak to her again.

As Jana made her way to the cafeteria for lunch later that afternoon, she met Funny Hawthorne. "Are you going to run for Miss Seventh Grade?" asked Funny. "If you do, I'll vote for you as long as you promise not to tell Laura."

Funny's question surprised Jana. She hadn't thought of herself as being popular outside of her own group of friends, let alone being well enough known to run for Miss Seventh Grade. *The Wigwam* yearbook was running its annual contest to determine who were the most popular kids in the seventh, eighth, and ninth grades at Wacko Junior High, as most kids called their school. The winners would receive their awards at a school assembly and have their pictures in the yearbook. Students who wanted to be candidates had to get fifty signatures and turn the list in at the office by Friday.

"Why would I run?" Jana asked Funny. "Kids wouldn't vote for me. I'm not that well-known."

"*What?* Lots of kids know you, and I've never heard *anyone* say anything bad about you." Funny hesitated and looked embarrassed. "Except for Laura, maybe."

Jana sighed at the mention of Laura McCall. She was the leader of a clique who called themselves The Fantastic Foursome. The Fabulous Five had had a run-in with The Fantastic Foursome on the very first day of school, and they had been rivals ever since. Besides Laura and Funny, Melissa McConnell and Tammy Lucero were members. Jana had heard that Laura made the other girls do things to belong, but she could never find out what, even though Funny and she had become friends. And Laura was always bragging that since she lived with her single father, she could do just about anything she pleased.

Funny giggled, breaking into Jana's thoughts about Laura. "I'm even starting a rumor that you and Randy Kirwan are going to run together as Mr. and Miss Seventh Grade," said Funny. "Everyone knows you're the perfect couple."

Jana's mouth fell open. "*Funny!* You're not *really* doing that, are you? Randy would make a super Mr. Seventh Grade, but there are lots of girls who are more popular than I am."

"Name one," demanded Funny.

"Why . . ." Jana thought for a moment. "There's . . . uh, Christie, and Laura, and what about you? You're so friendly. Everyone likes you."

"Christie doesn't like to be the center of attention. Remember how she didn't want to run for class president? And Laura? She's my friend, but I don't think that many other people like her as much as I do. She is kind of bossy.

"And me," continued Funny. "I guess people that know me like me, but I don't have nearly as many friends as you do. *Everyone* knows The Fabulous Five, and *you're* their leader."

Jana looked at Funny. She hadn't considered running for Miss Seventh Grade, but if Randy ran for Mr. Seventh Grade, it would be fun for them to run together. Randy was liked by everyone. He was the kindest and most sincere boy in the world, and he always stood by his friends. He had been the quarterback on the seventh-grade football team, and now he was on the basketball team, so everyone knew him. Maybe it was a good idea after all.

"I don't know," Jana said, still hesitating. "Maybe. But I'll have to think about it."

"Great! I'm taking that for a yes," said Funny. "I'll keep spreading my rumors, too. Gotta go," she said as they approached the door to the cafeteria. "If Laura sees us together, I'll have to explain why I was talking to you." She flashed Jana a big smile and waved with her fingers as she skittered away.

Jana didn't mention her conversation with Funny to her friends during lunch. Running for Miss Seventh Grade for the yearbook contest was such a new idea to her that she needed to think about it. If she and Randy both ran and won, being chosen together would be so romantic. Funny had said *everyone* thought they were a perfect couple. That thrilled Jana, even though she had secretly known it for a long time.

Jana waved to Shane Arrington as she entered her social studies class that afternoon. Shane looked a lot like River Phoenix and might be as popular as Randy, she thought as she settled into her seat. He was fun, played on all the seventh-grade teams, and was really laid-back. If Shane ran for Mr. Seventh Grade, he could have a chance to be elected.

Jana looked around for anyone else who might be competition as Mr. Broderick began calling roll. Curtis Trowbridge, who had gone to Mark Twain Elementary with Jana, was seated to the right of his girlfriend, Whitney Larkin. Whitney was a brain who had skipped sixth grade and gone right into seventh. She was smaller and shyer than the other kids. What about Curtis for Mr. Seventh Grade? Jana asked herself. He's seventh-grade class president so he's pretty popular. She shook her head. Although Curtis had won the election for president, neither Randy nor Shane had been running.

A movement near Whitney caught Jana's attention. Geena McNatt sat on Whitney's left, and Jana thought she had seen Geena pulling a folder from between two of Whitney's books. Jana couldn't be sure if that was what had really happened or if she had imagined it.

As the period passed, Jana couldn't keep her eyes from returning to Geena. Geena partially opened her notebook, and it appeared to Jana that she was looking at something in a folder, but had she really taken the folder from Whitney? Then Geena took out a blank page and wrote something on it. When she was finished, she dug a paper clip out of her purse and clipped it to the top of some papers she took from the folder.

Jana frowned. What was she doing? Just then, Geena glanced up and her eyes locked with Jana's. An arrogant look spread over her face, and she stuck her tongue out at Jana.

Jana could feel a hot flush creep up her neck.

"All right, class," Mr. Broderick said as the period drew to an end. "Please turn in the articles about pollution I asked you to cut out of newspapers and magazines over the weekend."

Jana dug into her notebook and took out her assignment. There had been another oil spill off the coast of Alaska, and it had been easy to find lots of articles in the Sunday papers. The only problem was, everyone else probably had the same ones. She had dug through some old *Time* magazines that were stacked under the coffee table in the living room and found a few others that were different. As she passed her assignment forward to Joel Murphy, who sat in front of her, she noticed Whitney frantically searching through her books.

Geena passed something forward and then gave Jana a mean look.

As they left the room, Geena walked up beside Jana and bumped her. "You tell, and I'll get you," she said, and then hurried down the hall leaving Jana staring after her with her mouth open.

CHAPTER

2

"**C**an you believe her nerve?" grumbled Jana, glancing at Geena McNatt, who was standing by herself near the old Wurlitzer jukebox in Bumpers. Jana was sitting in a booth with the rest of The Fabulous Five in the junior high hangout. "She actually took something from Whitney Larkin and threatened me if I told."

"Do you know for sure that it was Whitney's homework she took?" asked Katie.

"No, I can't prove it. I talked to Whitney after class, and she was almost crying. You know Whitney—the kids who went to Copper Beach Elementary with her say she's never made a grade lower than an A in her life. Not being able to turn in homework on time just blew her mind. She had cut out several articles about pollution, and if I know Whitney, she went to a lot of trouble to find some that no one else would have. But Geena could have gotten her own articles. Sunday's papers were full of them."

"What about the folder?" asked Beth. "Wouldn't that prove she took them?"

"Not if Geena doesn't have it anymore," said Christie. "And I'm sure she wouldn't keep it around for someone else to find."

"Why did she have to pick on Whitney?" said Melanie. "She's so shy."

Everyone nodded agreement.

"Do you suppose Whitney will tell Curtis what Geena did?" asked Katie. "If I know Curtis, he'll get *really* mad if he finds out."

"I told her I didn't think she should, and she agreed," said Jana. "Geena would probably run and tell her two brothers, and that would *not* be good for Curtis." Jana thought about the McNatt boys. Max was in the ninth grade at Wakeman and played noseguard on the varsity football team. He was rough and walked around looking as if he didn't like anyone. Joe was Geena's twin, but he was in the eighth grade instead of the seventh, and he was a slightly smaller version of Max. Jana had noticed Max sitting in a booth across the room with two other ninth-grade boys.

"What exactly did Geena say to you?" asked Katie.

"She said if I told, she'd get me," replied Jana.

Katie frowned. "That's not enough evidence to bring her before Teen Court. It would be your word against hers, and you can't prove it was Whitney's homework."

"I know." Jana poked at the ice in her soda. Since Katie was one of the student judges on Wakeman's Teen Court, she knew what she was talking about. "It's one thing for her to threaten me," Jana went on, "but I *really* hate to see her get away with what she did to Whitney. Whitney can't defend herself like most kids can."

"It doesn't look as if there's much we can do about it," said Christie.

"Changing the subject, how come your best friends are the last ones to find out the big news?" Beth asked, looking at Jana.

"What are you talking about?"

"Dekeisha Adams said that she heard that you and Randy were going to run for Miss and Mr. Seventh Grade in *The Wigwam* contest."

The others looked at Jana in surprise.

Christie almost knocked over her soda. "Is that true?"

"No. That's just a rumor that Funny Hawthorne is spreading," responded Jana.

"It sounds like a great idea to me," said Melanie.

"Why don't you do it? Everybody would vote for you."

"And it's not like running for class president or Teen Court," said Katie. "It's an honorary position, and you wouldn't have a lot of things to do once you were elected."

"And you and Randy are such a *great* couple," chimed in Melanie. "Oh, Jana! You just *have* to. We'll all help. You know we will."

Jana looked at each of her friends. They were *really* serious.

"Well, say something," said Katie. "Will you do it?"

"I might," Jana said slowly, picturing Randy standing next to her on the stage in the auditorium while they both waved to a crowd of Wacko Junior High students. "But only if Randy agrees to run, too."

"Fantastic!" squealed Beth. "We've got to have another meeting and make plans and posters like we did when Christie was running for class president."

"You mean when I *almost* ran," Christie said.

"Hey, wait a minute! Wait a minute!" Jana interrupted, holding her hands up to stop them. "I haven't talked to Randy about it yet. I don't even know if he'd be interested."

"Well, ask him," said Christie. "He's right over there."

"Not in here," said Jana, feeling instantly shy. "I'll talk to him tonight and let you all know in the morning." She looked at Randy, who was in an animated conversation with Keith and Shane. He was *so* handsome with his dark wavy hair and his wide white smile. He would make a perfect Mr. Seventh Grade.

"OUCH! Darn it!"

The shout startled Jana, and she looked around quickly. Geena and Clarence Marshall were squared off in front of the jukebox, and blood was dripping from Clarence's nose onto his sneakers.

"*You hit me!*" Clarence said angrily.

"Well, you shouldn't have shoved me!" retorted Geena.

"I didn't shove you. I just wanted to get to the jukebox to play a song."

"You did too shove me," Geena insisted, sticking her face into Clarence's as if she were a baseball player arguing with an umpire.

Jana saw Geena's brother Max bounce out of his seat and head to his sister's side.

"*Did you push my sister?*" Max snarled, jabbing a stubby finger at Clarence's chest. He was built like a small version of a refrigerator and was two or three inches taller than Clarence.

Clarence held his ground. "No, I didn't push her. I was just trying to get to the jukebox to play some music, and she stepped in front of me. Then she hit me."

"Let me hit him again!" yelled Geena, trying to get at Clarence.

Max pushed her away and puffed out his chest, and the look on his face got angrier.

Just as Jana thought he was going to hit Clarence, Shane Arrington stepped in between them.

"Hey, Max," Shane said in a friendly voice, as if he were oblivious to what was going on. "I was wondering if I could have your autograph."

A look of confusion came over Max's face. "My autograph?" he asked suspiciously, squinting at Shane.

"Sure," said Shane, putting his arm around Max's broad shoulders as if they had been buddies for a long time. "I was talking to Jana Morgan, and she and Funny Hawthorne are going to have a feature in the yearbook about the animals that some of the kids at Wacko collected money for at Christmas. Since you donated, they thought you'd be a good model for a reenactment."

Jana's mouth dropped open at what Shane was saying. It was true that she and Funny Hawthorne were seventh-grade coeditors for the yearbook, but they hadn't talked about a feature like the one Shane was telling Max about. She had seen Shane trick Max into donating money to save the animals. Was he trying to con Max again? She left her seat and went closer so she could hear better.

"Model? Reenactment?" asked Max. He had forgotten all about Clarence Marshall, who was wiping his bloody nose with the end of his shirttail and listening with interest to the conversation.

"Sure. You know how they do it when they want pictures of something that's already over," continued Shane. "They set up a reenactment and take pictures as if it were just happening. Since you were so nice about donating money, they thought you wouldn't mind having your picture taken at the collection table in the cafeteria." Seeing Jana nearby, Shane added, "Isn't that right, Jana?"

Not knowing what else to say, she nodded. "Yes, it is."

"See? What did I tell you, Max? And since you're going to have your picture in *The Wigwam* so many times, being a star football player and all, I thought I'd ask you for your autograph for my yearbook before everyone else did."

Max looked at Jana. The angry look had faded from his face. She shrugged and smiled at him.

Then, as if he had just remembered Shane was a lowly seventh-grader, Max winked at one of the ninth-grade boys he had been sitting with. "You'll have to stand in line."

"Okay," said Shane, smiling. "I just thought I'd ask." He walked away casually, but Jana saw him look around for Clarence, who had gone to sit with Joel Murphy.

A short while later, as she was leaving Bumpers, Jana caught up with Shane.

"You're such a con man," she said, laughing. "What would you have done if I had said I didn't know anything about doing a feature story on saving the animals at Christmas in *The Wigwam*?"

"Ducked," Shane responded with a big grin.

"That's twice I've seen you do that to Geena's big brother. The other time was when you tricked him into flipping a coin to see if he would donate to the animal fund, and he lost."

Shane looked at her with a twinkle in his eyes. "But you'll never be able to prove I tricked him, will you?"

They had walked along together for several blocks when Jana noticed a frown cross Shane's face. "What's wrong?"

"Hmm?"

"You were frowning."

"Oh, I guess I was just thinking about Igor."

Jana braced herself for whatever was to come next. Igor was Shane's pet iguana and he was always making fantastic claims about him. He insisted that when he let Igor out of the house and he wanted to come back in, Igor would bang on the door with his tail. He also claimed that Igor had a stuffed dinosaur that he liked to sleep with. During the campaigning for class officers, Shane had brought Igor into Bumpers wearing a sign that was draped over the lizard's back that said IGOR FOR PRESIDENT, and he had even tried to use Igor as a substitute baby during a Family Living class project. Shane was the only person she knew who loved an iguana, and she was sure he was about to pull something funny on her.

"Okay," she said with an I-know-it's-coming-so-get-it-over-with sound in her voice. "What's wrong with Igor?"

"He's sick, maybe even dying."

His words hit her like a cold wind. She waited for Shane to break into a smile and tell her that he was kidding, but he didn't.

CHAPTER

3

"Igor may be *dying*?" Jana asked incredulously. "Come on. Be serious. You're kidding me, right?"

"No," said Shane. "Something really bad is wrong with him. He just lies in his box and he hasn't eaten in three days."

"Have you taken him to a veterinarian?"

"They don't know anything about iguanas."

"What about the zoo?"

"My dad took Igor to the zoo, and they told him how to mix some mashed worms with a little medicine they thought might help. He wasn't interested in eating it either, but we pushed it down his throat with the eraser end of a pencil. He hasn't gotten any better, though."

Jana felt her stomach lurch at the thought of mashing worms.

"Does he have a fever?" she asked, changing the subject quickly.

Shane looked at her quizzically. "I don't know how to take an iguana's temperature, do you?"

"You put a thermometer in his mouth, maybe?" she asked hopefully, then shook her head, knowing that sounded dumb.

"Actually, they're cold-blooded animals so I don't think it's the same as with a dog or cat," said Shane.

Jana was about to suggest that, if lizards were cold-blooded animals, maybe the closer Igor's temperature was to freezing, the healthier he was. But that didn't make much sense either.

"Can Igor have visitors?" she asked.

Shane looked at her, obviously pleased. "Sure. Do you want to see him?"

"Why not?" Even though she was going along with the conversation, Jana was still half-afraid that Shane would break out laughing and tell her it was all a joke.

They walked the extra blocks past Jana's apartment building in silence. When they reached his house, Shane pushed the door open and let Jana enter in front of him.

She looked around the room as he shrugged off his jacket and hung up hers in the closet. The walls of the living room were covered with posters, similar to ones Jana had seen in news stories about the 1960s.

There were lots of flowers and peace symbols, and others were blown-up pictures of crowds of people with long hair and headbands milling around or standing on street corners. All the men had beards and wore patched jeans, and the women were mostly dressed in long, loose dresses and had flowers in their hair.

The furniture in the room consisted mainly of large pillows thrown around on the floor, a couple of low tables, and an expensive-looking stereo. Jana's eyes were drawn upward. The ceiling was covered with Styrofoam cups that looked like little blunt-nosed stalactites.

"It's my dad's idea of how to improve the acoustics," said Shane, noticing her upward glance. "He listens to his old records in here. Come on. Igor's in my room." He led the way down a hall.

Shane's room was totally different from what Jana had seen of the rest of the house. It was neat and had pictures of baseball and football players on the walls. Over his desk was a photograph of a man and a woman who could have come straight out of one of the sixties posters in the living room.

"That's my mom and dad," he said when he saw Jana looking at it.

It was obvious where Shane got his good looks. His mother was a thin, pretty lady, with long, brown hair. She was very young in the picture. His father was tall, with chiseled features, and a black beard.

Igor lay quietly sunning himself under a heat lamp in a box filled with sand and rocks in one corner of the room. There were two plants that looked like miniature potted trees wedged in between rocks, and a plastic pan of water was sunk in one corner like a little pool. All Igor needs is sunglasses and a swimsuit, Jana thought, holding in a giggle. It looks as if he's posing for an advertisement for a Florida vacation.

The greenish-brown iguana was over two feet long and lay so still she would have thought he was dead except for an occasional blink of his black eyes and the throbbing of the folds of skin under his throat as he breathed.

"He hasn't moved in the last two days," said Shane.

"Have you fed him anything different that might have made him sick?" asked Jana.

"Just the mashed worms and medicine."

Jana scrunched up her nose at the thought of the horrible mess. "Anything else besides that gourmet meal? He hasn't gotten out when you weren't looking, has he?"

"No," Shane answered, shaking his head.

Jana thought hard. She wished that she could think of something that would help, but she was certainly no expert on iguanas.

"How about a soda?" asked Shane.

"I don't think you could get him to drink one," said Jana, laughing.

"I don't mean for Igor, dummy. I mean for us."

Jana followed him into the kitchen, where the walls were painted a bright red and hung with more peace posters.

Shane opened the refrigerator to get out the sodas, and she saw that it was mostly full of health foods. He had once said that his mother and father ate a lot of fruit and things made with grains, and drank homemade vegetable juices. Shane took out an apple and offered it to her.

"Aren't you afraid that Max McNatt is going to catch on to you someday?" Jana asked as they sat at the table drinking the cola and eating apples. "He and his brother Joe might beat you up."

"I don't know what you mean," Shane said in a perfectly serious voice. "Max and I are buddies." The twitching at the corners of his mouth showed he was having a difficult time not smiling.

"You may think you are, but one of these days he's going to catch on to your tricks."

"Oh, Max is all right," said Shane. "He just likes to pretend he's tough. He wouldn't hurt anyone."

"His sister is a lot like him," said Jana. "Except she's not as big."

Shane looked at her. "Geena? What's she been doing?"

"She picks on people who can't defend themselves, like Whitney Larkin."

"I guess she does take after her brothers," said Shane.

They were still sitting at the table talking when Shane's mother and father came home, and he introduced them to Jana. She had been dying to meet them since she knew they had been hippies, and she had heard all sorts of things about them, such as how Mrs. Arrington used to bring rice balls and chopsticks instead of cupcakes to school for Shane's birthday when he was in the lower grades.

Mrs. Arrington was still pretty and had a sweet, almost angelic smile, but she had gained weight since the picture in Shane's room was taken, and her stomach was round. As she walked into the room, she was letting her hair down from a bun, and it fell to her waist.

Shane's father still wore a beard, although it was neatly trimmed, and his hair was long in back and gray at the temples. He was wearing a pin-striped suit.

"Let me at that fridge," said Mr. Arrington after saying hello to Jana. He tossed his suit coat carelessly over the back of a chair and took out a large pitcher that was full of an unidentifiable gray-looking liquid and filled a glass.

Jana watched in fascination as his Adam's apple bobbed up and down with each swallow. All he needs is a mole on his cheek and he would look like Abraham Lincoln, thought Jana.

"Care for some carrot and cucumber juice?" Mr. Arrington said, holding the pitcher out to Jana. "I made it myself."

Jana shook her head. "No thanks." The drink was probably nutritious, but if it tasted anything like it looked, she didn't want to gag in front of Shane's parents.

"I've got to go," Jana said, getting up. "I've got lots of homework tonight."

Shane walked her to the door. The Arringtons' old orange Volkswagen Beetle with flowers and butterflies painted on the sides sat in the driveway.

"I'm really sorry about Igor. I hope he gets better soon," Jana said to Shane. "And by the way, your parents are very nice."

He smiled. "They're different, but they're all I've got."

After dinner, Jana's stepfather Pink volunteered to help her mother with the dishes, and Jana went to call Randy before tackling her homework.

"Hi," she said when Randy answered. "Have you heard the rumor about me running for Miss Seventh Grade?"

"Yes," he responded. "I was going to ask you about that. When did you decide to do it?"

"I haven't actually," she said, laughing. "Funny Hawthorne is the one who made the whole thing up. She says that she thinks you and I would make perfect Mr. and Miss Seventh Grade. Katie, Christie, Beth, and Melanie said they thought so too, and they're pushing me to run."

"I think you'd have a good chance of winning. I

don't know a nicer girl in the entire class, but of course I'm prejudiced."

The sound in his voice made warm fingers dance up and down her spine.

"That's nice of you to say," she answered in a soft voice. "But I told my friends that the only way I would do it was if you would run for Mr. Seventh Grade."

The other end of the telephone line was quiet for a moment as Randy thought about what she'd said. Jana held her breath as she waited. It wasn't so much that she wanted to be Miss Seventh Grade. It was more that she wanted for Randy and her to be Mr. and Miss Seventh Grade together. It would be so perfect.

"If you really want to," he finally said. "I wouldn't do it either if you weren't going to run. That's the only way it would mean anything to me."

Jana thought she would faint with happiness. Randy had said yes! She couldn't wait to tell the rest of The Fabulous Five.

CHAPTER

4

"Randy said he *would* run for Mr. Seventh Grade if *I* would run for *Miss* Seventh Grade!" Jana almost squealed the news to the rest of The Fabulous Five as she joined them by the school fence the next morning.

"Fantastic!" said Christie, jumping up and down.

Melanie rolled her eyes back in her head. "Oh! You'll make the *dreamiest* Mr. and Miss Seventh Grade."

"Plans! We've got to make plans," shouted Beth. "The election is next Wednesday."

"Don't get excited, everybody," said Katie, putting her hands up as if she were a traffic cop. "We'll handle it. The first thing Jana and Randy have to do

26

is register their names in the office. That means we have to get fifty signatures for each of them first."

"Right," said Christie. "Everybody take two sheets of paper and write 'Jana Morgan for Miss Seventh Grade' on one, and 'Randy Kirwan for Mr. Seventh Grade' on the other, and get kids to sign them."

"We'd better ask if they've signed some other Fab Five's petition, though," said Melanie. "Duplicates won't count."

Jana grinned and nodded. It was great to know that she had such super friends. They were really excited about her running. "We'll compare petitions at lunch and strike out duplicates."

Christie jumped up and down. "We've got to have a planning meeting!" she chirped excitedly. "And we need to include the guys in on it."

"We could have a planning meeting at *my* house," Beth added. "Except if all my brothers and sisters are home, we won't be able to hear each other talk."

"We can have it at my house," Melanie chimed in.

"Okay. We'll meet at your house," said Jana. "At least until your parents get tired of our having our meetings in your family room." Suddenly Jana remembered something else she had wanted to ask her friends. "Did any of you know that Igor is sick?"

"Igor?" Christie asked, raising her eyebrows. The others looked at each other with concern showing on their faces.

"Shane didn't say anything to me," said Katie. "I

was talking to him yesterday afternoon in social studies."

"He told me after we left Bumpers yesterday," said Jana. "Then I went over to his house to see Igor, and he *didn't* look good. Shane said he hasn't moved in three days."

"How does a sick iguana look?" asked Beth. "Was Igor all green around the gills?"

"He always looks green around the gills," said Katie. "That's his natural color."

"Oh, yeah," Beth said.

In spite of the fact that she did care about Shane's pet, Jana giggled. "I couldn't see any difference in his color. Someone his dad talked to at the zoo told him to feed Igor mashed worms with some medicine that he recommended."

"*Eee-YEW!*" said Melanie, screwing her face into a funny expression. "That's gross!"

Christie stuck her tongue out as if she were going to throw up. "*Ugh!*"

"Shane's really worried," said Jana, frowning. "He told me he thought Igor might even die."

"Oh, no!" said Beth with a look of horror. "What would he do without Igor?"

"Maybe we should send Igor get-well cards," said Katie. "It might cheer Shane up."

"And we could wear yellow ribbons to show we're pulling for him," suggested Christie.

"That's what we did for Randy when he was in the hospital," complained Jana.

"That's all right," responded Christie. "Randy deserves as much consideration as Igor does."

Jana's mouth dropped open. Then she saw the twinkle in Christie's eyes as she nudged Katie. Christie was teasing her.

"Okay. Those are great ideas," said Jana, laughing. "Let's tell everyone we know and get them all to do the same thing. Tomorrow morning everybody show up with yellow ribbons on."

"All *right*!" shouted Melanie.

After English class Jana met Randy in the hall, just as she did every day. She was so excited about The Fabulous Five's plans for getting them both nominated, she filled him in right away. "And here are my petitions for you and me," she added, showing them to him, "and you've got to sign in the space I left right below my name. Oh," she said, remembering. "First I'm supposed to ask if you've signed anyone else's petition for us."

"No," Randy said, laughing. "Wow! You must have fifteen names already." He took her notebook and scribbled his name where she'd pointed.

"Unless there are a lot of duplicates, I wouldn't be surprised if we got the fifty signatures today."

"It's kind of nice to know that you've got so many friends," he said, handing the petition back to her.

*   *   *

Jana was surprised to see how fast the word had spread about Randy and her. Dekeisha Adams, Sara

Sawyer, Mona Vaughn, and lots of other people stopped her in the hallway between classes to tell her they would vote for her and Randy. Garrett Boldt, who was in the eighth grade and was the photographer for the yearbook, told her that he wished he could be in the seventh grade for just one day so he could vote for her. Even Taffy Sinclair, who had been Jana's worst enemy at Mark Twain Elementary, smiled sweetly and told her that, since *she* didn't have time to run for Miss Seventh Grade herself because of her busy modeling schedule, she would vote for Jana.

Jana watched Taffy walk away holding hands with Cory Dillon, the lead guitar player with the student rock group, The Dreadful Alternatives. She couldn't help remembering how The Fabulous Five had once started a club against Taffy Sinclair at Mark Twain Elementary. Taffy had been so snotty then and was always trying to steal Randy Kirwan away from Jana. While Taffy was still something of a show-off, she was going with Cory now, and she and Jana were getting along a lot better at Wacko Junior High.

When Jana walked into the cafeteria at lunch period, the first person she met was Curtis Trowbridge. "I heard the news about you and Randy running for Mr. and Miss Seventh Grade in *The Wigwam* contest. As you're probably aware, as seventh-grade editor of the newspaper, I have to maintain an unbiased position." Then he adjusted his black horn-rimmed glasses, winked slyly, and said, "But frankly, I'll be pulling for you."

Jana smiled to herself. Curtis was the world's biggest nerd. His straight hair always seemed to have a cowlick standing up in back, even though he obviously tried to plaster it down with something sticky. She had been saved from the mad crush he had on her in elementary school when he met Whitney Larkin at Wakeman.

As Jana made her way through the lunch line, other kids stopped to congratulate her and tell her they would vote for her and Randy. Even Clarence Marshall, who was always a pain, said he would vote twice for her. Three times if she would give him her dessert. By the time she had made her way to where The Fabulous Five were sitting, she had talked to at least twenty people who said she had their vote.

"Jana, we think we've got enough signatures already," Beth said excitedly.

Katie and Christie each had four sheets of paper placed side by side in front of them and were checking names as they ate their lunches. "We're comparing lists to see if there are any duplications," mumbled Katie around a mouthful of yogurt.

"Here's mine," said Jana, dropping her petitions next to the others. "Have you heard about anyone else running?" she asked Beth and Melanie.

The two of them shook their heads.

"I did hear that Chet Miller is going to run for Mr. Ninth Grade," said Beth.

"And I heard that Shelly Bramlett and Daphne Alexandrou are running for Miss Eighth Grade," said Melanie.

"Gee, I don't know which one I'd vote for," said Jana. "They're both nice."

"Seventy-five names for Jana," said Christie. "And no duplications."

"And seventy-five for Randy," said Katie.

"It's not surprising since everyone who signed for Jana signed for Randy, too," said Beth. "When kids think of Jana, they think of Randy and vice versa. Instead of waiting until Friday, you can turn the petitions in today."

Heather Clark and Melinda Thaler stopped at the table. "You and Randy have got my vote," said Heather.

"From what I hear, there doesn't need to be an election," said Melinda. "You and Randy will win easily."

Alexis Duvall stopped by to give her support, too. Jana noticed Geena McNatt, who was by herself as usual. She was drinking a carton of chocolate milk and came up to stand behind Katie as if to eavesdrop.

"Is it true you and Randy are going to run for Mr. and Miss Seventh Grade?" asked Alexis.

"We've got the petitions with seventy-five names on them right here," said Katie, pointing at the papers spread out on the table in front of her.

Christie tossed the papers she had been checking on top of Katie's.

"Those are the petitions?" asked Geena, reaching over Katie's shoulder to spread the papers with one hand as she sucked on the straw stuck into her chocolate milk.

Jana nodded and turned back to speak to the others. "I don't think Randy and I—"

"Look out!" cried Katie. Chocolate milk was running down her front and splashing all over the petitions.

"Oh! I'm *so* sorry," said Geena, sweetness dripping from her voice.

Jana dabbed at the brown stain on Katie's shirt with her napkin while Katie and Christie grabbed the petitions and shook the milk off them.

Jana stared at Geena in disbelief. Had she spilt the milk on purpose? While Geena said she was sorry, Jana could swear her eyes had a twinkle in them. Jana took a napkin offered by Melanie, and when she turned around again, Geena was gone.

CHAPTER

5

"Can you *believe* that Geena McNatt!" Katie cried angrily as she held her shirt away from her body so the chocolate milk would dry. "My top is *ruined*."

"It was probably just an accident," said Christie. "Why would she want to spill milk on you?"

"I don't know, but that's exactly what she did."

"You two haven't had an argument, have you?" asked Melanie.

"No, we haven't had an argument," answered Katie. "I've never even talked to her. There's no reason for her to be mad at me."

Jana looked at her friend's shirt. Chocolate stain ran all the way down from her left shoulder to her waist. "You'd better go to the girls' room and soak it

34

or else it will never come out. I've got a clean T-shirt from gym in my locker. I'll get it and bring it to you."

"While you two do that, we'll clean up the petitions," volunteered Christie. "They may be a mess, but I think Miss Simone will accept them."

As Jana hurried down the hallway to her locker, she thought again about the look in Geena's eyes. No matter what she said, she didn't *seem* sorry about the accident. But Katie had said she hadn't had any problems with Geena. What other reason could there have been? Maybe it really was an accident. Jana felt sorry for Katie. It would be embarrassing wearing the gym shirt all afternoon.

"I hear you and Randy are running for Mr. and Miss Seventh Grade," said Marcie Bee, whose locker was next to Jana's. She was taking out some books for her next class.

"Yes, we are," Jana replied as she dialed the number on her combination. She hoped that Miss Simone, the principal's secretary, would accept the messed-up petitions. It would be a pain to have to ask all those kids for their signatures again.

"Yeek!" Jana gasped, and felt a shock wave at what she saw when she opened the door.

"What's wrong?" Marcie asked as she yanked Jana's locker door farther open so she could see.

Jana couldn't get out a single word. All she could do was point. Inside her locker the clothes hanging from the hooks were covered with a red mess that was dripping down on her gym shoes. The books and notebooks lying at the bottom of the locker looked even worse. They were drenched in the thick red substance.

Gingerly Jana picked the sleeve of her jacket up with two fingers and examined it closely. It looked too thick to be blood. She sniffed it. It smelled like tomato. *It was catsup.*

"Oh, no, not you too," exclaimed Marcie. "I just saw Mona Vaughn and Whitney Larkin. Someone had squirted that icky red stuff into their lockers, too. It was all over their clothes and books. Who could have done such a thing?"

"I'm not sure," Jana murmured. Angrily, she pushed aside the jacket to check the white gym-suit shirt she had promised Katie. There was a small smear of catsup on the tail. It could be washed and the damp spot wouldn't show when it was tucked in, but that wouldn't make Katie feel any better. She was mad enough already at having the chocolate milk spilt on her. Jana's shoes and the two books she had tossed in the bottom of the locker were worse off. They were drenched in the icky red stuff.

Jana leaned against the door of her locker with the soiled shirt in her hand. Why had someone squirted catsup all over her things? Whoever it was must have taken one of the squeeze-type catsup bottles from the cafeteria to do it. The pointy spout would fit perfectly through the louvers in the locker doors. That meant it had been planned.

The thought shocked Jana, and a sinking feeling settled in the pit of her stomach. She had been feeling so happy. Everyone was saying she and Randy were so well-liked that they would be a cinch to win the Mr. and Miss Seventh Grade contests. Someone certainly doesn't like me, she thought. I don't know for sure that it was Geena, but who else could it be?

She took the gym shirt from its hook and hurried to the girls' room to give it to Katie.

Katie was still fuming when Jana got there, and the catsup on the shirt didn't help her temper. She was so angry when Jana explained what had happened that her face turned almost as red as her hair.

"That girl is a bully," Katie snarled as she patted the wet spot where the catsup had been with a paper towel.

"I don't know for sure that she did it," said Jana, trying to sound reasonable even though her emotions kept telling her the sneak catsup squirter had been Geena.

Katie stopped patting the wet spot and looked up at her. "Can you think of *anyone* else who might have done it?"

"No, I can't. But remember, you're the one who is always saying we have to be fair, and until we have proof, we can't convict her."

Katie sighed and tucked the still-moist shirttail into her pants. "There are some times when it's harder to be fair than others."

"There's one thing I haven't told you," said Jana.

Katie raised her eyebrows questioningly.

"Someone squirted catsup in Mona's and Whitney's lockers, too."

Katie waved her finger in the air. "What did I tell you? Who else would have done a thing like that to the three of you? You're on her list."

"Well, if we're on her list, why would she want to spill chocolate milk on you? You said you hadn't even talked to her."

"I *don't* think she intended to spill the milk on me," responded Katie.

Jana stared at her friend. "Well, if you think it was an accident, why are you so mad? That's not like you."

"I didn't say I thought it was an accident. I said, I didn't think she intended to spill it on me. What I think is, she wanted to spill the milk on your petitions. I think she's after you, and that's what makes me mad."

Jana's jaw dropped open. "*Me?* Why me? Just because I might have seen her take the folder from Whitney Larkin? That doesn't make sense. Whitney hasn't turned her in. She can't prove Geena took her homework."

"I don't know what her reasons are," said Katie. "But I think you had better watch out for her."

Jana stared at her friend. It didn't make sense. Was Geena *really* doing these terrible things on purpose? Neither Jana nor Whitney had done anything to make Geena mad at them. There had to be an explanation. But try as hard as she could, Jana couldn't think of one.

CHAPTER

6

*J*ana flattened her petitions on the office counter as well as she could as she and Randy waited for Miss Simone to finish her telephone conversation. Christie, Beth, and Melanie had wiped most of the chocolate stain off of them while she was getting the gym shirt for Katie, but the papers were badly wrinkled and some of the names that were written in ink were smeared.

"What can I do for you two?" asked Miss Simone, hanging up the telephone and coming to the counter.

"We'd like to file these petitions for *The Wigwam* Mr. and Miss Seventh Grade contest, if they're not too messed up," answered Jana. She was tempted to explain why they were so wrinkled, but she didn't.

There wasn't any use stirring up things any more than they already were.

Miss Simone took the papers, and Jana could see a smile dancing at the corners of her mouth as she counted the names. "All the signatures are still legible, but we'll need to check them for duplicates. However, I think these will be just fine. I'll let you know if there are any problems."

"Thanks!" Jana and Randy said in unison.

"Uh, Miss Simone. Has anyone else turned in a petition for the seventh-grade contests?" asked Jana.

"Let me see. No, not yet."

"Thanks again," said Jana, giving her a big smile.

"Just think!" Jana said to Randy when they were out in the hall. "What if no one else runs? Then they wouldn't have to have an election for the seventh grade."

"Yeah," Randy agreed. "But if no one else runs, what does it prove? It certainly wouldn't mean we're the most popular boy and girl in the seventh grade. Besides, I'm not sure I want to know how popular I am. Being popular doesn't mean you're the *best* person."

Jana looked up at him. He was serious. "I agree," she said, nodding. "If we win, it would just mean we have a lot of friends. I know a lot of people that I think are at least as good as me. Katie is so fair and honest; Christie is brainy and popular; Beth is always taking up causes to help people, like the American Indians; and Melanie is so sweet, and she's the

one who wanted to save the animals at the shelter."
Jana looked into Randy's eyes. "And then there's
you. You've got to be the kindest, sincerest person I
know."

Randy's face turned a light shade of pink, and Jana
giggled. "You're blushing," she said.

"It's nice that you think so," he said, looking embarrassed, "but I don't think I can live up to that
kind of publicity." Then his eyes softened, and he
said, "It's great that you think so."

Jana floated down the hall on her way to her next
class. Randy was fantastic. She felt lucky to be
going with him.

As she turned a corner, she slammed into Geena
McNatt. Both girls' books scattered across the floor,
and Jana grabbed at the wall to keep from falling.

"*You did it again!*" shouted Geena. "Don't you *ever*
look where you're going?"

"*Me?*" Jana was shouting back. "I was just walking
like any normal human being."

"*Are you saying I'm not normal?*"

Jana had never seen such anger in a person's eyes.
She struggled to regain control of herself. She wasn't
going to let Geena drag her into a fight. That wasn't
the way people solved problems. "Look," she said.
"It was just an accident. Let's forget it."

"It's easy for you to forget, *Miss Popularity*," Geena
shot back. "Just because you and your friends think
you run the school doesn't mean you can run over
people in the hall."

Jana stared at Geena in shocked disbelief. "What are you talking about? I don't think that my friends and I run the school."

"Yes you do!"

Jana drew in a deep breath and looked at the angry girl standing in front of her. She was taller than Jana by a couple of inches, and she was dressed in the same oversized red sweats she always seemed to be wearing. Jana wasn't afraid of her, but she couldn't understand her at all. It was as if she were a volcano waiting to blow.

Calmly, Jana began to pick up her books. Two other kids who had stopped to watch the argument handed her a notebook and two social studies books. One of them was Geena's, and Jana held it out to her. Geena snatched it from her hand.

Jana brushed off her skirt and turned to leave. As she walked away, she could feel Geena's eyes burning into her back.

CHAPTER

7

$\mathcal{M}$elanie stood in the middle of the Edwardses' family room and banged a pen against her soda glass. "Okay, everybody. It's time to put the puppies back in their box so that we can start our meeting."

Groans filled the air.

"Oh, come on, Mel," said Jana. Melanie's family had adopted a dog named Rainbow from the local animal shelter. A few days later, Rainbow had had eight puppies. Now Jana was cuddling two tiny puppies under her chin. "We can talk and hold puppies at the same time."

"Oh, yeah? That's what you think. We wouldn't get a thing done," she countered. "This is important. Put the puppies back."

44

Reluctantly, Jana placed the puppies close to Rainbow, who had been stretched out in the box quietly watching The Fabulous Five play with her babies. In fact, Jana had been sure that she had been smiling. One by one the others replaced the little dogs, who began climbing all over Rainbow. One fat little puppy who was exactly the same mixture of colors as his mother began tugging on one of her ears.

Melanie looked down into the box and then back at her friends. "Okay. Who's hiding one? There are only seven here."

"Not me," said Jana. "You all saw me. I was the first one to put mine back."

"Me, neither," said Randy, holding his arms wide in a gesture of surrender.

Everyone else shrugged and glanced around, looking innocent, until Christie put her hands on her hips and said, "Okay, Calcaterra. Why is that lump in your shirt moving?"

"Who? Me?" he said. Then he grinned sheepishly. "Oh, yeah. It is moving, isn't it? Must have been something I ate."

"Don't tell me that Mr. Macho is really just an old softie," quipped Katie.

Everyone laughed at that, and Tony unbuttoned his shirt and drew out a brown bundle of fur, which he deposited in the box with the others.

Melanie clanged her glass again. "Before the

meeting starts, we have something special to do,"
she said.

Randy, Shane, Scott, Keith, Tony, and Jon looked
at each other questioningly as Jana and Christie dug
behind one of the couches and brought out the paper
bags The Fabulous Five had hidden there earlier.
Jana and the other girls each reached in and pulled
out small bows made from yellow ribbon and gave
one to each of the boys. Then Melanie passed
around a small tin box that contained safety pins to
the girls.

"These ribbons are to show our concern for Igor,"
said Jana as she pinned one on Randy's shirt and
then her own. "And you're supposed to wear them
to school every day until he's well."

"They're kind of like the ones the kids wore for
Randy when he was in the hospital," observed Jon.

"There is a resemblance between Randy and
Igor," kidded Keith. "In fact, they could be related."

Randy threw a crushed potato-chip bag at him.

"And that's not all," said Beth. "We also have get-
well cards for Igor." The girls pulled cards from
their notebooks and purses and handed them to
Shane.

"Tell Igor we care," said Katie.

For a minute Shane just looked around the room
without saying a word. Jana could tell from the look
in his eyes that he was moved by his friends' concern.

"I know Igor will appreciate it," he said finally.

"You won't mind if he doesn't send you thank-you cards until he gets over whatever he has, do you? I don't think he's up to it yet."

"How's he doing?" asked Jon.

Shane shook his head. "Not good. I still can't get him to eat, and I don't think he has moved two inches since last week."

"What about asking Mr. Dracovitch to look at him?" asked Randy. "He knows a lot of things about biology."

Jana wished she had suggested the same thing to Shane when she was at his house on Monday. Mr. Dracovitch was a biology teacher at Wakeman and he acted pretty weird sometimes. He wore a black wig that made him look like a vampire, but he only did it to interest kids in taking his science classes.

"That's a good idea," answered Shane. "My dad and I've asked everyone else we can think of."

"Now to get on with our business," said Melanie, taking the center of the room again. "We're here to officially start the Jana Morgan and Randy Kirwan campaigns for Mr. and Miss Seventh Grade, and you've all been chosen to serve on the campaign committee."

"Not another campaign," said Scott, putting both hands over his eyes.

"How much is it going to cost us this time?" asked Tony.

"Only some of your time and talent, which isn't worth much to begin with," said Katie, laughing.

"I'll remember that the next time Mr. Bell sends me to Teen Court, Your Honor," Tony responded. "See if I make it easy on you judges by pleading guilty again." Everyone except Katie laughed that time, but she punched him on the arm.

"Listen up!" commanded Melanie loudly. "We've got poster boards and Magic Markers. Let's get to work or we'll be here all night."

Shane stood up and saluted Melanie as if she were an officer as everyone took one of the sheets of poster board and chose bright-colored Magic Markers.

While Jana thought about what to put on her poster, she looked around at the group of friends and thought about how hard they were working to help her and Randy run for Mr. and Miss Seventh Grade. They were all wearing their bright-yellow ribbons and chattering happily to each other. Geena's accusation that Jana thought she and her friends ran the school was absolutely false. She wouldn't have thought about running for Miss Seventh Grade if Funny Hawthorne hadn't started the rumor that she was going to. And then the rest of The Fabulous Five started telling her that she should run. Randy was right though. Just because you had lots of friends who might vote for you, it didn't make you better than anyone else. But it also didn't make you any worse. So why did Geena think so badly of her? It made her head spin trying to figure it out.

*   *   *

The next morning, Jana and her friends raced through the halls before school putting up the posters. By the time the bell rang for homeroom, they had finished. Besides the posters for her and Randy, she had seen posters for Kaci Davis, Marsha Reel, Chet Miller, and D. J. Doyle for ninth grade and Daphne Alexandrou, Shelly Bramlett, and Garrett Boldt for eighth grade. Jana was glad to see that someone had talked Garrett into running. She would have to tell him that she wished she could be in the eighth grade for one day so she could vote for him. There were still no posters for anyone else who was in the seventh grade.

During the day, Jana was swamped with people wanting to tell her that they were glad she was running, and they would vote for her. Twice, as she talked to groups of kids, she saw Geena McNatt staring coldly at her from a distance.

As she hurried into her social studies class that afternoon, she spotted Shane wearing his yellow ribbon, and the kids sitting near him were talking to him about it. Good, she thought, straightening hers a little and sticking out her chest to show it off, maybe some others will start wearing them, too.

Jana slid into her chair and waved to Mona Vaughn, who was sorting through makeup and other odds and ends she had taken out of her purse. Jana smiled at the bottle of bubble mix that was among the things spread out on the top of her desk. Mona's family couldn't afford a pet, so she managed to save money from her lunch allowance to buy the bubble mix, which she took to the animal shelter some days after school. She would blow bubbles into the cages of the dogs and cats, and they would chase and bite at them. It was Mona's way of making the animals happy until someone came to take them home.

At that moment Geena McNatt came down the aisle. When she reached Mona's desk, she stopped and picked up the bubble mix and shook it. "Baby stuff," she said with a sneer and dropped it. Mona had to grab for the bottle to keep it from rolling off onto the floor as Geena took her seat.

How could Geena be so mean? thought Jana, shaking her head. It was no wonder no one paid any attention to her when she hung around. And she dressed so sloppily. All the other girls wore things that made them look attractive and most put on some makeup, but Geena wore baggy sweats that looked terrible on her and she never seemed to comb her hair. No boy would *ever* ask *her* out.

I guess I should feel sorry for her, thought Jana, but it's hard. The best thing probably is to ignore her. She's really just a pain, but I can put up with it.

Mr. Broderick called the class to attention and began the day's lesson. As the lecture droned on, Jana's attention was pulled back to Geena. She had a ruler and was using it to slowly push the books on the corner of Mona's desk off the edge. Mona was concentrating so hard on what Mr. Broderick was saying that she didn't notice what was happening.

Jana watched, frozen for a few seconds. Should she warn Mona? Before she could decide what to do, the books went crashing to the floor.

Mona nearly jumped out of her chair, and Mr. Broderick stopped speaking as everyone turned to see what had happened.

Mona's face turned bright red, and she scrambled to pick up her books. "Sorry," she said in a tiny voice.

The teacher cleared his throat and began again.

As the lecture continued, Jana watched Mona peek over her shoulder at Geena, who smiled at her sweetly and waved her ruler.

Geena really is a menace, Jana thought angrily. First she took Whitney Larkin's homework, and now she's knocked Mona's books onto the floor. I don't mind her picking on me. I can handle her, but why does she have to pick on people like Mona and Whitney? *Something had to be done about Geena McNatt.*

CHAPTER

8

"*S*he *deliberately* knocked Mona's books off her desk," Jana said angrily. She, Katie, and Beth were on their way to Bumpers together after school.

"Not to mention her knocking you down once in the school yard and almost running over you in the hall," said Beth.

"And then she spilled the chocolate milk all over me and the petitions," Katie added.

"I know," said Jana. "But I really think the two times she ran into me were accidents. She's just rough and careless. I don't know if she spilled the milk on purpose or not, but what she did to Mona and Whitney was *definitely* on purpose."

"And don't forget the catsup that got squirted on

the stuff in your locker," said Katie, brushing her windblown hair out of her face.

"I didn't *actually* see her do that," responded Jana. "And why would she want to pick on me, anyway? If you can give me a good reason, I might understand it."

"Because she thinks you saw her take Whitney's homework, and she wants to intimidate you," said Katie. "Besides, who else is there to suspect?"

Jana shrugged. "I can't believe that's the reason. It has to be *more* than that."

"Being just plain mean must be in the McNatts' blood," said Beth. "Max and Joe are both rough, and most of the other guys stay out of their way. I don't know their older brother, George, but I'll bet he's just like them."

Melanie and Christie were drinking colas and sitting in one of the brightly painted carnival bumper cars that had given Bumpers its name when Jana, Katie, and Beth arrived. Melanie quickly undraped her legs from over the front of the car as she and Christie hopped out to join them in a booth.

"Well, how's the future Miss Seventh Grade of Wacko Junior High?" asked Melanie.

"I haven't won yet," answered Jana. "Have you heard yet whether anyone else is running?"

"I haven't," said Christie. "But I can't believe that Laura McCall won't sign up."

"Me either," said Katie. "She'll run just because

Jana's running. She won't be able to stand it if Jana gets elected Miss Seventh Grade."

"I haven't heard of any other seventh-grade boys running either," said Melanie.

"All the most popular ones are friends of Randy's and won't run against him," said Beth. "I know Keith wouldn't, and I don't think Shane, Tony, Scott, or Jon would either." The others nodded agreement.

"I've been talking to everybody I see about voting for you," said Christie. "They all say they will."

"Me, too," said Melanie, and the others said they had been also.

"Oh, look!" cried Christie. "There are Dekeisha and Marcie Bee, and they're wearing yellow ribbons."

Jana turned to see the two girls coming through the door and waved. Each one had a bright-yellow bow pinned to her jacket. "That's neat. I hope more kids wear them."

Just then Jana saw Geena McNatt slip through the door and stroll casually over to the Wurlitzer jukebox and stand by herself. Jana couldn't help wondering why Geena came to Bumpers anyway. She was always alone because she didn't have any friends. She never sat with anyone. Mostly she just hung around looking totally out of place.

"Look at that, will you," said Christie, giggling.

Jana did a double take and broke out in laughter. Coming through the door were Clarence Marshall and Joel Murphy, and they were both wearing yellow bows, only theirs were made from wrinkled ribbon that was at least four inches wide and covered half of their chests. Clarence and Joel had big grins on their faces and strutted in among the bumper cars and tables showing off their ribbons as if they had just won first place in some big contest.

"Well, what do you think?" asked Clarence when they got to The Fabulous Five's booth. He pushed his messy hair out of his eyes. "We found this ribbon in a garbage can outside the art room."

"I'd say you've got the spirit," said Melanie. "No matter how wrinkled your bows are, you can't miss them."

"It's the thought that counts," said Joel. "Igor is one of our favorite people, and we thought we'd show that we care about him, too." He made a half-hearted attempt to stuff his dangling shirttail into his jeans but failed, and the two of them continued their promenade around the room.

As The Fabulous Five sat and talked, Jana noticed several other yellow bows around the room. There were a lot of people who cared about good old Igor, she thought.

"Now, look at *that*," gasped Katie, pointing toward the door again.

Jana turned again, expecting to see another yellow ribbon since there had been a regular parade of kids coming through the door with them on. Instead she saw Mona Vaughn come in and head directly for the girls' room. It looked as if she was crying.

Jana heard Melanie say, "What in the world!" behind her as she slipped out of the booth and hurried after Mona.

Jana found her washing her face. "What's wrong, Mona? Can I help?"

"Nothing," Mona said, trying to suppress a sniffle.

"It doesn't look as if it's nothing to me," Jana said, digging into Mona's purse to find a tissue.

"Yeeek!" cried Jana, jerking her hand back out and holding it up as sticky stuff dripped off the ends of her fingers. "What's *that*!"

"Bubble mix," answered Mona, wiping at her eyes with the back of her hand.

Jana wiped her hand on a paper towel and cautiously opened the purse wide. Inside, the gooey liquid covered Mona's wallet, papers, pencils, and all the other things she kept in her purse. It looked as if it were some strange stew and it smelled like soap. "Is that the bubble mix you take to the animal shelter?" Jana asked as she touched the tip of one finger in the fluid again to test it.

Mona nodded.

"Did the lid come off?"

Mona shook her head solemnly.

"What *did* happen?" Jana asked.

Mona looked at her. "Geena McNatt grabbed my purse, and I tried to get it back, but she wouldn't let me have it. Then she took the bubble mix out and dumped it inside."

Jana stared at Mona openmouthed. She felt hot anger rise up inside her, and the hair stood up on the back of her neck. She was madder than she had ever been. Spinning on her heel, she burst out of the girls' room and looked for Geena. She was going out the door.

Jana dodged through the tables and bumper cars and ran after her, catching her as she was starting down the street.

"Geena McNatt, that was the most despicable thing you've ever done!" Jana shouted. "Mona Vaughn saved her lunch money to buy that bubble mix so she could play with the animals at the shelter, and you had to *waste it* and ruin the things in her purse on top of that! Don't you have any sense?"

Geena first looked surprised, and then fire came into her eyes. "It's none of your business! *I didn't do anything to you, did I?*"

Jana heard someone come out of Bumpers behind her. "I'm not sure about that!" she said. "I think you squirted that catsup in my locker, for one thing. And you may have squirted it in Whitney's and Mona's lockers, too, and you spilled chocolate milk on Katie and on Randy's and my petitions on purpose!"

"What are you saying to our sister?" a boy's voice asked.

Jana turned and was facing Max and Joe McNatt. She looked back at Geena, and Geena was grinning.

CHAPTER

9

Even though Jana was surrounded by McNatts, she stood her ground. "Your sister is a menace! She stole Whitney Larkin's social studies homework, knocked Mona Vaughn's books off her desk, squirted catsup in a bunch of lockers, and now she's dumped bubble mix into Mona's purse!"

Joe McNatt looked at her contemptuously. "I don't want you to say things like that about our sister," he drawled. "She doesn't do things like that."

"Yes she does!" insisted Jana.

Geena pushed her way in between her brothers. "Just because you think you're some *big deal*, running for Miss Seventh Grade, doesn't mean you can go around accusing people of things. You and your friends don't run Wakeman!"

"Run Wakeman?" That was the second time Geena had said that. "We don't run Wakeman," Jana insisted. "We've never said we did."

"Well, you act as if you think you do!" Geena retorted, her eyes shooting fire.

"Hey, Max! What's going on, friend?" Shane strolled into the middle of the argument with a sideways smile on his face.

Max reached out and grabbed Shane by the front of his shirt and shoved him against the wall. "Don't get funny with me, Arrington! You're one of the baby seventh-graders who thinks he's a big deal."

"Whoa!" said Shane, spreading his hands to show he didn't want to fight. "You've got it. I'm no big deal. I'm just a lowly Wacko seventh-grader."

"Remember that!" said Max, giving Shane one last push before letting go of his shirt.

"I don't think you ought to do that." Tony Calcaterra's voice was so soft and low Jana barely heard him. He, Randy, Keith, and Jon had come out of Bumpers, and the rest of The Fabulous Five were right behind them. Tony was almost as tall as the ninth-grader, and the intensity of the expression on his face surprised Jana.

Max and Joe stared at Tony and then looked at the other boys who had encircled them.

"Come on!" Max snarled, shoving Joe and grabbing Geena by the arm and pulling her after him.

Jana hadn't realized she had been holding her breath until she let out a "Shooo!" and felt herself shaking.

Randy put his arm around her. "You didn't have to take on the whole McNatt clan by yourself, you know," he said teasingly.

"I know," she said. "But I was so mad that I couldn't think."

"What did she do to Mona?" asked Katie.

After Jana explained what had happened and the boys had gone back inside, she looked at her friends and asked, "Could we have an old-fashioned Fabulous Five meeting at my house?"

They all nodded.

Soon Christie and Melanie were sprawled on Jana's bed, Katie sat in the chair at her desk, and Beth sat cross-legged on the floor of Jana's room. They each had a soda and were munching on potato chips. Seeing them in her room this way made Jana feel as if they were back at Mark Twain Elementary at one of their weekly Against Taffy Sinclair Club meetings.

"This is how I feel about it," said Jana, standing in the middle of the room. "Geena McNatt is *truly* a menace. I didn't mind so much when it seemed as if she might be mad at me, but when she picks on people like Mona Vaughn, and spills the bubble mix Mona takes to the animal shelter in her purse, Geena has gone *too far.* Mona has to save every penny she gets to buy that bubble mix."

The others solemnly agreed.

"I've got a proposal," Jana continued. "We need to get evidence to prove that Geena is doing nasty things to people so we can take her to the Teen Court. Then she can be punished, and everyone will know what kind of person she is. I think we should come up with a plan for one of us to be watching her as much as possible."

"What can the Court do to her?" asked Melanie.

"It depends on the seriousness of what she's done," answered Katie. "If we could prove that she stole Whitney's homework and squirted catsup in the lockers, that's pretty serious. The Court might make her do work around the school, or they might even put her on probation. If she did something worse after that, they could recommend that she be suspended from school for a few days."

"Wow," said Jana. "We'd better be pretty careful. That's serious stuff. I wouldn't want her to get into that kind of trouble unless she really deserves it."

"What kind of evidence do we need?" Christie asked.

"Well," Katie said, raising her eyebrows as she thought. "It has to be something besides our word against hers. That would just seem as if we were picking on her. I heard what she said about you, Jana, thinking you were a big deal because you're running for Miss Seventh Grade and us believing we run Wakeman. It's not true, but she might try to get other people to believe it. They won't know how we had to twist Jana's arm to get her to run for Miss Seventh Grade."

"And *I* sure don't want to run Wakeman," said Christie. "I've got enough trouble running my own life."

"Everybody knows you talked Curtis Trowbridge into running for class president so you wouldn't have to," Beth said to Christie, laughing. "That shows how badly *you* want to be a big deal."

"That's not the way Geena sees it, though," said Jana. "And what she says might sound logical to someone else. If we don't handle it right, *we* could turn out to be the bad guys instead of her."

"We have to have *hard* evidence that she has done something wrong," said Katie. "And I'll have to disqualify myself from the Teen Court if we accuse her of something. I'm one of The Fabulous Five, so she'll claim I'm prejudiced, and she'll be right."

"The first thing we have to do is figure out her class schedule so one of us can be where she is at all times," said Jana. "Is Geena in anyone's homeroom?"

"Mine," answered Melanie. "Why don't I follow Geena to *her* first class, then I'll tell *Christie*, who's in *my* first class, what room Geena's in, and she can tail *Geena* to *her* second class. Whew!" Melanie flopped back on the bed as if she were exhausted.

"Oh, good," said Beth, jumping to her feet. "Can I wear a mustache and a trench coat when I follow

her? I'll even wear my sunglasses so she doesn't rec-
ognize me."

Katie slapped the heel of her hand against her
forehead. "It would be just like you to do something
like that."

"Beth," said Jana, smiling at her dramatic friend,
"I think your everyday school clothes will do just
fine."

"Remember the notebooks we had when we went
to Mark Twain Elementary, and we were keeping
notes on Taffy Sinclair because she was so snotty?"
asked Christie. "Why don't we each keep a notebook
again, and then we can get together and compare
notes?"

"Great idea," said Jana.

At dinner that evening, Jana poked at her food
while her mother and Pink talked.

"You're not eating your dinner, Jana," her mother
said. "Aren't you feeling well?"

Jana looked up and smiled reassuringly at her.
"I'm fine. I was just thinking."

"A deep-dish, pepperoni, green pepper, and
mushroom pizza for your thoughts," teased Pink.
He knew that was her favorite kind of pizza.

"I was just thinking about how some people see
other people differently from the way they see themselves."

"Deep thought," said Pink.

"Yes, it is, honey," said her mother. "Do you have
a problem?"

Jana looked at the two adults who were the most important people in her life. Even though Pink, which was short for Wallace Pinkerton, had only been her stepfather for a few months, he had dated her mother for a long time before that and had seemed like part of the family. The two of them were always there when she needed them, and they knew her better than anyone else, even better than The Fabulous Five. "Do you think I act as if I'm a big deal?" she asked.

"Oh, no, honey," said her mother, putting her hand on Jana's. "I think you're just about the most levelheaded young lady I know."

It's nice to hear her say it, but she *is* my mother, thought Jana. But what if she *was* acting like a big deal the way Geena had said? Was it possible? Wouldn't Randy Kirwan, who was the nicest, most sincere person in the world, notice it if she were? He wouldn't like her anymore if it were true. The thought made Jana shudder.

Why did Geena have to pick on people? And why was she so angry at Jana? Most people didn't act that way. Was it something Jana had done without realizing it, or was it true that bad blood ran through some people as Beth had said? And then there was that terrible confrontation outside Bumpers. Jana had been in a fight, and yet she didn't completely understand why. It was like a bad dream with things happening that didn't make sense. Would she wake up soon and everything would be okay?

CHAPTER

10

*T*he next day in the cafeteria Melanie put her food tray on the table next to Jana's and snapped off a sharp military salute. "Secret agent Mel Edwards reporting, ma'am."

Jana laughed and said, "At ease, Agent Mel," and then she turned serious. "Did you see Geena do anything bad to anyone?"

"No," Melanie said, sliding into her chair. "She hit Clarence Marshall on the back of the head when she ran by him once, but other than that she didn't commit any TC offenses."

"'TC offenses'? What's that?" asked Beth, who was sitting on the other side of the table.

"*Teen Court*, of course," answered Melanie. "Here

comes Christie. Let's see if she has anything to report."

Christie dodged through kids as she made her way to them.

"No," she said in answer to their query. "I followed her from one end of the school to the other between first and second periods. Gosh, her classes are far apart. She didn't have time to stop and pick on anyone if she was going to be on time. Katie was supposed to follow her between her next classes."

The results were the same when Katie reported in. "Only I think she might have seen me following her. She looked over her shoulder a couple of times, and I tried to act as if I had business being where I was. I don't know if I fooled her or not."

"What you need, my dear, is Madam Beth Barry's secret-agent disguise kit. It's only nineteen ninety-five postage paid," said Beth, holding a napkin over the lower part of her face and sounding mysterious. "It's guaranteed to fool your own mother. It's so good, *you* won't even know who you are."

"Get serious, Beth," Melanie said, laughing. "You're ridiculous."

"Well, we don't have any TC offenses on her yet," said Jana. "And if she knows we're following her, we may not be able to get any."

"What on earth does 'TC' mean?" asked Katie.

"It's Mel's term for Teen Court," Jana answered.

Katie put her hands over her eyes. "I should have known it was something Edwards thought up."

"I'll try to follow her after lunch," said Jana. "Geena's in my social studies class, and it will seem natural to her if I'm headed in the same direction as she is."

"Try following in front of her," said Melanie. "That's what they do in the private-eye shows on television."

"How can I watch what she's doing if I'm in front of her?" asked Jana.

"Look in your mirror while you're walking," Melanie suggested.

"And run into every kid in the hallway?" Jana responded.

"It wouldn't be bad if they were boys," Melanie shot back.

"I think Melanie's just found a new way to spend her afternoons," said Katie. "Walking through the halls at ram speed running into boys."

Melanie stuck her tongue out at Katie, and the others laughed.

When the first bell rang for class, Jana stood on her toes and peeked through the bobbing heads of the people walking in front of her. She could see Geena's reddish-brown head not too far away. She was sure Geena hadn't seen her yet, and if Jana stayed far enough behind, maybe she could keep it that way. The social studies classroom was down the hallway they had just passed, so Geena must be going to her locker first to get her books.

Abruptly Geena stopped and looked back.

Jana quickly bent her knees and dropped down into what must have looked like a duck walk so she wouldn't be seen. Two eighth-grade girls were staring at Jana as if she had totally flipped. Jana pasted a goofy smile on her face and acted as if she were flicking ashes from a cigar, saying, "Just practicing my Groucho Marx routine."

She raised her head cautiously and saw that Geena had started walking again. When Geena stopped at her locker and started working the combination lock, Jana hurried past and crossed the hall to stand at the end of a row of lockers where she could watch Geena and duck out of sight if she had to. Also, she would be behind Geena again when she headed back to the social studies class.

Geena opened her locker and reached into the bottom to pick up a book, giving Jana a clear view of the shelf at the top. Jana's eyes opened wide at what she saw there, and she slumped against the wall behind her, nodding her head in satisfaction. There it was—the evidence she needed to take Geena before the Teen Court where she could be punished for at least some of the mean things she had been doing. Jana smiled to herself. She had an idea about how to get the evidence out of Geena's locker, too.

CHAPTER

11

"*J*ana!"

Jana waited for Funny Hawthorne to catch up with her as she watched Geena go into the social studies classroom.

"Jana, *have I got news for you*," said Funny. She was all smiles, as usual.

Jana loved Funny's bubbly personality. It was what made her want to be friends with Funny in spite of the fact they belonged to rival cliques.

Funny looked over her shoulder as if to see who might hear and then said, "Laura isn't going to run against you in the Miss Seventh Grade contest. With everyone talking about you and Randy and no one else running, she won't say it, but I know she thinks she doesn't have a chance of beating you if no one else enters."

Jana knew that Funny liked Laura a lot, but she must really be Jana's friend, too, for her to tell her about Laura. "I'm glad. I really didn't want the contest to be a battle between The Fabulous Five and The Fantastic Foursome. *You* know who's the *real* cause of my being in the contest in the first place."

Funny giggled and covered her mouth. "Me!" she said merrily. "Not that I don't think Laura's super. She's a good friend. I just think that you and Randy will be *the* perfect Mr. and Miss Seventh Grade."

"We haven't won yet."

"The deadline for registering is tomorrow," responded Funny. "I'll bet no one else in the seventh grade runs. Wouldn't that be great? Got to get to my next class. See you." She waved with her fingers and hurried off.

During class, Jana kept an eye on Geena. She looked as though she was concentrating on what Mr. Broderick was saying and taking notes, except for one instance when she turned and smiled at Jana.

Jana was stunned. Why had Geena smiled at her? Did she want to be friends all of a sudden? It didn't seem like that kind of smile.

After social studies, Jana hurried toward the yearbook office. At that moment, it was more important for her to try to catch Garrett Boldt than to follow Geena. Jana knew that Garrett stopped in *The Wigwam* office in the afternoon to deliver pictures he had taken or to get another assignment, and she had to see him before school was out for the day. She was in luck. When she entered the room filled with work-tables and a large bulletin board with notes and schedules pinned to it, she found him sorting through some papers.

"Garrett, is your camera difficult to operate?" she asked.

"No. Not really," he said, pulling several large photos out of an envelope. "Why? Do you want to become a photographer? I'll take pictures of you when you get elected Miss Seventh Grade if that's what's worrying you. You won't have to do it your-self."

"Silly. That's not why I'm asking. I wondered if your camera is simple enough for me to take pictures with and if I might borrow it. I wouldn't even take it out of the school building."

"I'll take the pictures for you, if you want," he offered.

"I kind of wanted to take these myself. I only need a couple. But thanks a lot," Jana added quickly.

Garrett put his camera bag on the table and opened it.

"Uh-oh. That's a big lens. Is it hard to use?" Jana asked.

"The zoom? No, it's not. It lets you take close-up pictures from a distance. Do you want to use it?"

"That would be perfect," said Jana. "Would you show me how it works?"

Jana felt like a real spy. She had asked if she could leave her last class of the day early to go to the bathroom, and now she had the camera with the zoom lens tucked under her jacket and was peeking around the corner at Geena's locker. She looked at her watch. There were still three minutes before the last bell of the day.

Jana raised the camera and peered through the viewfinder, which was what Garrett had called the little window at the back that you looked through to see what you were shooting. The long lens was heavy and wavered a little as she tried to hold it still. Slowly she turned the ring on it. Geena's locker door seemed to come magically closer until the louvers at the top filled the viewfinder. Then she turned another ring and the image sharpened until she could see runs in the paint on the door. Amazing! she thought.

RINGGGG!

Jana jumped at the sound of the bell ending the last class. Soon kids started straggling into the hallway in ones and twos and then in groups. Locker doors clanged as they opened and closed them, putting books in and taking sweaters, coats, and books out. Jana covered the camera with her jacket and watched for Geena.

Shortly, Jana saw her coming down the hall. She was loping along and carelessly bumping kids on the way. Geena quickly dialed the combination of the lock on her locker and flung the door open. There *it* was, still standing in the same place on the upper shelf.

As Geena tossed books into the bottom of the locker, Jana swung the zoom lens up and homed in on the object sitting on the shelf. Perfect, she thought, and pushed the button. The whirring sound of the automatic rewind on the camera startled Jana, and her heart jumped into her throat. She looked around quickly to see if it had attracted anyone's attention. It hadn't.

Next she turned the ring on the lens, just as Garrett had shown her, and the picture in the viewfinder enlarged to show all of Geena and the locker. The object inside was still very clear. Jana smiled to herself as Geena turned to show her profile and Jana snapped another picture. Perfect evidence, she thought, and feeling suddenly professional, she took three more pictures before returning the camera to the inside of her coat.

Jana watched as Geena slipped on an oversized jacket, which probably had belonged to one of her brothers. Then she kicked defiantly at the books lying on the bottom of her locker.

Well, Miss Geena McNatt, thought Jana, we'll see just how much you can get away with now.

CHAPTER

12

*A*fter she left Bumpers, Jana dropped off the roll of film at the one-hour photo shop. Katie and the others had agreed that the pictures of the squirt-type catsup bottle sitting on the shelf in Geena's locker, along with the testimony of Mona and Whitney about catsup being squirted into their lockers, was pretty good evidence. Jana was going to call Marcie Bee about testifying that she'd seen the catsup on Jana's jacket, too. All in all, Jana was satisfied that she had covered all the bases. She was feeling so good that she ran the last half block to her apartment.

There was a strange car sitting outside her apartment building when Jana turned into the walk, but she dismissed it. Its driver could be visiting anyone in the building.

As she hung up her coat in the hall closet, she could hear her mother and a man talking in the living room. Curious, she picked up her books from the table and went in to say hello.

But as Jana stepped into the living room, she froze in her tracks. The smile on her face suddenly felt pasted there. Sitting on the couch next to a very burly man was Geena McNatt.

"Come sit down, Jana." Her mother's stiff voice broke the silence that had fallen over the room. "This is Mr. McNatt, and I'm sure you know Geena."

Jana crossed the room cautiously, as if it were a pool filled with piranhas and sat on the edge of the chair next to her mother.

"Mr. McNatt has been telling me about some trouble that you and Geena have been having at school," her mother continued. "I told him I was sure there is a logical explanation for it and that things could be worked out." Everyone's eyes were on Jana.

Mr. McNatt's face was square, like the rest of his body. His hair was light colored with flecks of gray and was cut short like Max's and Joe's. In fact, he looked like Max, only grown up. His eyes peeked out of the puffy flesh around them, but Jana was surprised to see that they didn't look all that unkind.

"Geena says that you've been picking on her, Jana.

She says that you started a fight with her outside Bumpers and blamed her for Mona Vaughn's having bubble mix in her purse, which she says she had nothing to do with. She also says that you and your friends have been following her around school."

"My brothers will tell you she started the fight, too!" Geena interrupted.

Her father put his hand on her knee to quiet her as Jana's mother continued, "As I told you, Mr. McNatt, I'm sure my daughter can clear up the whole matter. Do you want to tell us what's happening, Jana?"

Jana felt as if she were sitting in a witness chair and there were a spotlight centered right on top of her head.

"Geena *did* spill the bubble mix in Mona's purse. Mona told me she did."

"Why did you automatically assume this other girl was telling the truth and that my daughter did it?" Mr. McNatt asked in a gravelly voice.

"I've known Mona for a long time, and *she wouldn't do something like that*. Besides, I saw Geena knock Mona's books off her desk," Jana said.

"So you've taken the side of a friend against someone you don't know as well." Mr. McNatt stated it as if he were a judge ruling on a criminal offense.

"No. That's not it at all," Jana protested, looking to her mother for support. "Geena has been doing lots of bad things to people. She took Whitney

Larkin's homework, and she squirted catsup in my and some other kids' lockers, and—"

"*Did you see her do all these things?*" Mr. McNatt demanded.

"I saw her take Whitney's homework."

"Can you *prove* it?" Geena joined in the cross-examination.

"No! But I saw it." Jana was getting scared. No matter what she said, they didn't seem to believe her.

"My daughter doesn't lie, Mr. McNatt." Jana's mother's voice sounded as crisp and hard as his had.

He raised his hand. "I'm sure she thinks she's telling the truth, Mrs. Pinkerton, but sometimes what we see isn't always what happened. We just need to come to an understanding."

"And she thinks she's such a big deal because she runs around with that group that calls themselves The Fabulous Five, and she is running for Miss Seventh Grade!" snapped Geena. "She thinks she can run over anybody she wants."

"Now, Geena!" Her father silenced her with a frown. "That's not going to help a thing."

Turning to Jana's mother, he said, "I believe that what we have here is a failure to communicate. I'm sure your daughter is a very nice young lady, and I know mine is. Ever since my wife died when Geena was three years old, I've had to be both mother and father to her and her brothers. Believe me, I run a tight ship.

"Now," he said as if he had reached a conclusion that they should all listen to. "I think the two girls should get to know each other better. That's the first thing I do when I go out to one of my construction sites. I get to know the men, and they get to know me, and everything is hunky-dory from then on. If they don't like my rules, I fire 'em," he chuckled. "But they know I'm a fair man. Why don't you girls try spending a little time together. It might do you some good to get to know some other people, Geena. And you, Little Miss," he said to Jana. "It might help you to meet some people outside of this group you call . . . what's their names? The Fabulous Five? It will help broaden your understanding of people. Make you a better person."

Jana sank back into her chair and shivered in her anger. She didn't *need* to broaden her understanding of people. She *knew* that The Fabulous Five were the most wonderful friends in the world, and that Geena McNatt was a bully. *He didn't understand at all!* Tears bubbled up in her eyes, and she fought to keep them from falling.

"I don't agree with your total assessment of the situation, Mr. McNatt," said Jana's mother. "I do, however, agree that if Jana and your daughter get to know each other better, it might help. I'm sure they will *both* reevaluate their actions after this afternoon," she said, looking at Geena.

Mr. McNatt got up and touched his fingers to his forehead in a symbolic tipping of his hat to Jana's mother. "We'll be going now. It's been nice to meet you both. Don't take it too hard now, Little Miss. These things go away with time," he said, smiling and putting his hand on Jana's shoulder warmly.

Jana watched as her mother walked Geena and her father to the door. She couldn't believe it. Not only was she being picked on by Geena McNatt, but now Geena was making it look as if Jana was the bully. It was totally unfair.

CHAPTER

13

Jana's mother's face was full of anger when she walked back into the room.

"Mom, I'm not picking on Geena! Honest!"

Her mother's face softened. "I *know*, sweetheart. You would never do a thing like that. It's obvious, however, that Mr. McNatt totally believes his daughter, too." She reached out and took Jana's hand. "Come on. Let's sit down and talk about this."

The tears finally leaked out as Jana told her side of the story, and her mother put her arm around her comfortingly.

"Was I wrong to bawl Geena out in front of Bumpers?" Jana asked.

"No, you weren't." Her mother looked thoughtful

for a moment. "I just wonder what makes Geena do those things. Her father seems like a nice enough man. Still, there has to be a reason why she acts the way she does. What do you think it is?"

The thought startled Jana. A reason for Geena's picking on Mona and Whitney and squirting catsup in lockers? She was starting to believe that it was just because she was mean. "I don't know," Jana mumbled.

"Well," said her mother, getting up, "it's something for us to think about. Right now I need to get supper started. Sloppy joes okay tonight?"

"Yum," said Jana. "Do I have time to bike over to One-Hour Photo?"

"I think so, but don't be too long. Oh, by the way. Don't forget tomorrow's Pink's and my bowling night. You'll have to order a pizza."

Jana nodded and bit back a smile. As if she could forget that Friday night was bowling night. Her mom and Pink had been going bowling on Friday nights since they had started dating when Jana was a little girl. She wondered how many hundreds of deep-dish, pepperoni, green pepper, and mushroom pizzas she had consumed on Friday nights.

As Jana pedaled along, an idea began nibbling at the back of her brain, and it was full grown by the time she reached the photo shop. She thumbed through the pictures she had taken with Garrett's camera as the clerk stood watching. They had turned out terrific. "How much would it cost to get

a couple of these made into eight and a half by
eleven inches?" she asked.

The clerk gave her the price, and she calculated
what she would have with the money in her bank at
home and her allowance, which she would get tomorrow. It would be more than enough. "I'd like
this one and this one enlarged."

Jana hummed to herself on the return trip home.
The nerve of Geena, lying to her father and bringing
him to Jana's house to tell stories to her mother. As
her mother had said, Geena seemed to have her father convinced she was a nice girl. Her mother was
right about another thing, too. Something was definitely wrong with that girl, and Jana knew what it
was. She had a terminal case of meanness. Well, if
Geena's father was as nice as Jana thought, she might
just have a way of showing him what his daughter
was *really like*.

"I asked at the office," said Christie at noon the next
day, "and no one besides you and Randy has signed
up to run for Miss and Mr. Seventh Grade. You're
home free!"

"*Yea!*" cheered Katie, Beth, and Melanie. The
Fabulous Five raised their milk cartons in a salute.

"Can you imagine?" said Beth. "That's awesome."

"Does your majesty want anything from this
lowly servant?" said Melanie, bowing her head to
Jana. "A quart of blood? My head? Anything?"

"Quit fooling, guys," said Jana. "After what Geena said about my thinking I'm a big deal, I'm not sure I want to be Miss Seventh Grade. Other people might get the same idea about me."

"Hey. Don't let it bother you," said Katie. "She was just trying to make you feel bad. You're not that way at all."

"How could you be bigheaded when your best friends are so outstanding?" kidded Beth.

"Seriously. It bothers me," said Jana. "I've never had anyone say that to me before. It's made me stop and think. I do have the best of everything, you know. Randy is fantastic. You guys are the best. Everything is just so great. Do I show off without realizing it?"

"Hey, no," said Melanie, putting her hand on Jana's. "You're not that way at all. Why do you think everyone wants you to be Miss Seventh Grade? It's because you don't have a big head, that's why."

"Yeah, Jana," added Christie. "I've heard kids say they're going to vote for Marsha Reel for Miss Ninth Grade because they think Kaci Davis is stuck up. No one feels that way about you."

Jana looked at each of her friends' faces. They all wore concerned expressions. "Okay," she said, laughing. "I'm super. I just wanted to hear you say it."

Four wadded-up paper napkins hit her in the face at the same time.

*   *   *

Jana left Bumpers early that afternoon so she could go by the One-Hour Photo store and get the enlargements she had ordered. She was glad that Geena and her brothers were still there. So far everything was going according to her plan.

On the walk to the store, she thought about all the yellow ribbons that were being worn for Igor by seventh-graders. Girls were wearing them on their blouses and in their hair, and nearly every boy had picked up on it. Of course, good old Clarence Marshall was still wearing his huge ribbon, only now it was starting to get so smudged it didn't look very yellow anymore. It was funny, she thought, but it seemed to her as if Clarence was starting to hang around Geena a lot. He couldn't possibly be interested in a girl that had bloodied his nose, could he?

Jana's thoughts turned to Igor. She had talked to Shane at Bumpers, and he told her that he had put Igor in a box and taken him to Mr. Dracovitch, who took the iguana home to observe him for a few days and to try to get him to eat. Poor old Igor. She really hoped the science teacher could figure out what his problem was.

The enlargements were ready, and Jana paid for them and headed for Geena's house. Her father should be home from work by now, and if she was lucky, she could talk to him before Geena got there. She sighed. She'd have to do it, even if it meant having another confrontation with Geena and maybe even Max and Joe. But Mr. McNatt *is* a nice man, she told herself. I just *know* he is. If I can just get him to listen and look at these pictures, he'll know I'm sincere and will have to believe me.

Still, going to Geena's house was scary. She drew in a deep breath and turned the corner onto the McNatts' street.

CHAPTER

14

*J*ana punched the doorbell, drew in a deep breath, and squared her shoulders. The garage door at the side of the house was closed, and she couldn't tell if Mr. McNatt was home or not. She crossed her fingers behind her back.

A young man who was obviously a McNatt opened the door. He had the same blondish hair his father had, but he wore it longer, and his features were more delicate. He also had a light sprinkling of freckles across his nose like Geena. Jana guessed he was older than Max, probably high school age, and must be George. The last of the McNatts, thought Jana. Now I've met them all.

"Is Mr. McNatt home?" she asked as cordially as she could.

"If you mean my dad, no, but he should be here in about two minutes," the boy answered. "You can come in and wait for him if you want."

Jana was surprised at how pleasant he was. "Uh, no. I don't know if I should."

"Sure you should," he said, smiling and opening the door so she could enter. "You came to see him, and I know he'll be here shortly. I've got dinner just about ready, and he can smell it from *wherever* he's at. By the way, I'm George."

Jana laughed in spite of herself.

George showed her into the living room, and she sat nervously on the edge of the couch listening for sounds that would tell her if Geena, Max, or Joe might have come into the house from another direction. The only sounds she could hear were made by George in the kitchen, so they must still be at Bumpers.

Minutes passed and Mr. McNatt didn't come. Jana squirmed on the couch. The longer she waited, the more likely it was that Geena and the others would come home first.

Then she heard footsteps on the front porch and the doorknob rattled as someone turned it. Jana sprang to her feet, hoping against hope that it was Geena's father.

Max stepped into the room, and he and Jana stared at each other. A puzzled look crossed his face.

Geena pushed Max out of the way and barged in. "What's for sup—" When she saw Jana, she stopped dead in her tracks. "What are *you* doing here?"

Joe came in next and looked at Jana. To her relief he gave Max a shove, and the two of them went into the kitchen.

Jana clutched the envelope containing the photos close to her chest. "I came to see your father," she said as bravely as she could.

"My father? *Why?*"

Jana squared her shoulders and made her backbone straight and rigid. "Because I have something to show him." She heard a car door slam in the driveway.

"What do you have to show him?" demanded Geena.

"You'll see."

Geena glared at Jana as if she could eat her alive.

"Well, what do we have here?" asked Mr. McNatt as he stomped into the house. "What brings you here, Little Miss?"

Before Jana could answer and tell him about the pictures, he continued, "I'll bet I know." He waved a finger in the air. "You've thought about the trouble you and Geena have been having, and you want to be friends with my daughter, don't you? I *knew* as soon as I saw you that you were a fine girl yourself. Come on then," he said, reaching out and taking hold of her and Geena's arms. "Why don't you give your mother a call and stay for dinner?"

Jana was pulled into the kitchen where George was taking a big casserole of lasagna out of the oven, and Max and Joe were arguing over who should set the table. Mr. McNatt grabbed the two boys by the shirt collars and bumped their heads together. Max and Joe frowned at Jana as if she were the cause of their being punished.

"Quit the arguing! We've got company for dinner," their father ordered. Then, turning to Jana, he commanded, "There's the phone on the wall. Pick it up and dial your mother."

"Really, Mr. McNatt, I ought to . . ." As Jana tried to protest, he turned his back on her and went to the sink and started to wash his hands.

"Nonsense, Little Miss," he said over his shoulder. "If you and my Geena are going to be friends, you might as well start *right now.*"

Jana looked at Geena, who stared back.

Jana gulped and reached for the phone to call her mother. As she dialed, she heard Geena's father say, "George, you idiot, you burned the lasagna again."

Her mother sounded surprised at Jana's plans, but she said she was pleased that Jana was making an effort to be friends with Geena. Unfortunately there was no opportunity for Jana to blurt out the truth and ask her mother to rescue her from the McNatts without Geena's father's hearing. She sucked in a deep breath as she hung up the telephone and turned back to the dinner table, where the McNatt family was waiting expectantly for her.

The dinner was like nothing Jana had ever experienced in her entire life. Max and Joe battled each other for the lasagna and the garlic bread, and their father bellowed at Joe, who sat next to him, each time he reached across the table to get the Parmesan cheese.

"The five of us have been making do ever since the children's mother died ten years ago," Mr. McNatt explained to Jana. He jerked the lasagna platter away from Joe, who had jerked it away from Max, and handed it to Jana so she could have seconds. "We've done pretty well, if I do say so myself. The boys have been easy for me, of course. I know how to handle men. You just rap them across the head to get their attention. But Geena has been something else. She's a young lady. I'm real glad you've decided to be friends with her, Little Miss. For some reason, she doesn't bring any of her other girlfriends home."

Jana looked out of the corner of her eye at Geena, who was staring red-faced into her plate. She's embarrassed, thought Jana. Geena McNatt is actually *embarrassed*. Just then Max grabbed the garlic-bread basket. Seeing it was empty, he lunged for the half-eaten bread on the edge of Geena's plate. Jana watched in amazement as Mr. McNatt's long arm streaked out, and he hit Max on the back of the hand with the ladle from the lasagna before Geena even had time to react. Max jerked his hand back and rubbed his knuckles, and Geena flashed him a look of triumph.

"Geena looks a lot like her mother. She has her tiny freckles and wavy hair, only she doesn't keep it as neat as her mother did. But I suppose that will come when she gets interested in boys." Mr. McNatt looked at Jana hopefully. "Maybe you can give her some advice on how to dress a little more . . . feminine."

Geena's father really *doesn't* understand why she has no friends, Jana thought. It boggled her mind. She had to agree that after seeing the family up close, Geena probably wasn't too bad, compared to Max and Joe and even her dad. All of them, except George, who ate quietly by himself at the end of the table, were pretty rough. George seemed somehow to be different. She wondered if he was more like his mother than the other children.

After the meal, Mr. McNatt ordered Max and Joe to do the dishes so that Jana and Geena could spend some time together. Jana looked longingly toward the front door. The last thing she wanted to do was spend time with Geena, and she knew Geena felt the same way about her. If only there was some way to escape. But there wasn't—for either of them— and Geena led her silently up to her room.

The room was pretty much what Jana expected. Sweat suits and dirty tube socks littered the floor, and jeans were hung on the bedpost. She didn't see one piece of feminine clothing in the room. She would have liked to look in the closet to see if there were any there.

Geena stood to one side, chewing her lip while Jana looked around. Suddenly she snarled, "What do you have in that envelope? Is it something you're going to show my dad?"

Jana looked at her for a moment, thinking. "No," she said. "They're just some pictures I took with Garrett Boldt's camera."

Geena stared at her as if she didn't know whether to believe her or not. "Well, I guess you think you're really big time now that no one is going to run against you for Miss Seventh Grade."

"Look, Geena. I didn't want to run for Miss Seventh Grade. My friends talked me into it. I couldn't care less about it, except that Randy Kirwan is running for Mr. Seventh Grade, and I think it would be nice to run with him."

Geena sneered, "You've got all the friends in the world, don't you? I bet you make your Fabulous Five friends jump through hoops." She moved a picture of a pretty red-haired lady that was on a table that served as a desk.

"No," Jana said patiently as she moved toward the table. "As a matter of fact, I don't think *anyone* could make people like Katie Shannon and Christie Winchell do something they didn't want. They're pretty strong. We've just been friends a long time. Is this your mother?"

Geena nodded.

Jana picked up the frame and looked at the smiling, freckled face in the photo. "She's so pretty. Do you remember her at all?"

"It's none of your business!" Geena snapped.

Jana put down the frame and backed away a little. "I don't remember much about my father," she said softly. "He's not dead, but my mother divorced him when I was little. He's an alcoholic, and I write to him sometimes, but he hardly ever answers."

Geena squinted her eyes and stared at Jana, as if trying to decide whether or not to believe her.

"You're lucky to have such a nice dad," said Jana. "He really loves you. I can tell."

Geena shrugged. Suddenly her face seemed to soften. "Are you going to have a new dress for when you win Miss Seventh Grade?"

"I hope so," Jana said. "But I'm not sure. Listen, I'd better go. Randy's coming over tonight, and we're going to listen to records."

All at once the sparks flew back into Geena's eyes, and she turned away. Jana mumbled good-bye, but Geena didn't respond.

As Jana was making her way down the stairs by herself, Geena called out in an ominous tone, "You'd better take care of that dress."

CHAPTER

15

*L*ater that night, after Randy had left, Jana got into bed and sat up in the dark, thinking. After eating at the McNatts' house that night, she was amazed to find that she felt sorry for Geena. It must be awfully lonely for Geena, being a year older than everyone in her class, hanging around the edges of groups, and going to Bumpers by herself. And everyone in her family, except her older brother George, seemed to solve things by hitting or yelling. Even Mr. McNatt, who was a construction supervisor, had to be tough to handle the men he worked with. Maybe Geena had never seen any other ways of solving her problems. There had to be a way to help people like that.

But what about all the kids Geena picked on? Jana asked herself stubbornly. Feeling sorry for Geena probably wouldn't stop her from bullying people. And even though Jana had tried to talk to Geena about her mother, Geena had threatened her about the dress. Jana sighed. Geena McNatt was a bully. That's all there was to it.

Jana was still sitting up and thinking when she heard her mother and Pink come home. Her mother pushed the bedroom door open slightly and peeked in.

"Oh! You're still awake, sweetheart. How was your dinner?"

"Okay. Mom, can I talk to you a minute?"

"Sure." Her mother turned on the bedside lamp and sat on the edge of the bed. "What's up?"

After Jana told her about her supper at the McNatts' and her conversation with Geena, she asked, "Can you and Pink do me a favor?"

"Sure, sweetheart. What is it?"

Jana told her about the plan she had just come up with and the part she needed her mother and Pink to play in it. Her mother's expression turned from quizzical to pleased as she listened.

The next day was Saturday, and since no one else could enter the competition for Miss Seventh Grade, and Jana was assured of winning, her mother announced that she and Pink wanted Jana to have a new dress for the awards ceremony. Jana found a beautiful dress with a creamy gold top and buttons that matched the dark blue skirt. Her mother even let her pick out a necklace and matching earrings to go with the outfit. Jana couldn't wait to wear it.

Later in the day, she called the rest of The Fabulous Five and asked them to come to her house. That was when she told them about her plan and asked for their help, too.

On Monday, just about everyone in the seventh grade at Wacko, except Laura McCall, Tammy Lucero, and Melissa McConnell, seemed to tell Jana how glad they were that she and Randy were going to be Mr. and Miss Seventh Grade. Even Kaci Davis told her how she envied Jana's not having to wait until the voting on Wednesday. Jana saw Geena McNatt staring at her several times with an angry look on her face when people were congratulating her.

"You won't believe how gorgeous my new dress is," Jana told a crowd of girls who had gathered around her in the hallway after lunch. As she described the dress to "Oohs" and "Aahs," she watched Geena out of the corner of her eye. She was drifting around the outside of the group pretending not to be listening, but each time Jana went into detail about some part of the dress, Geena would stop and turn an ear toward her.

On Tuesday, after school at Bumpers, Shane climbed onto a chair, put his arms up, and asked for everyone's attention. "I want you all to know how much Igor has appreciated all the cards that he has received and the yellow ribbons that everyone has been wearing to show their concern for him during his illness. On the advice of a close friend, I asked Mr. Dracovitch if he would have a look at Igor."

Several kids booed at the mention of Mr. Dracovitch's name.

"Our illustrious teacher has been able to do what the veterinarians and the people at the zoo were not able to. He has discovered the cause of Igor's affliction, so you can all take off the ribbons."

A cheer went up throughout Bumpers, and some of the kids pounded on the tables. "Igor! Igor! Igor!" someone started chanting, and the others picked it up. Mr. Matson, the owner of Bumpers, stood beside the cash register and smiled.

Shane let the cheering continue for a moment before he waved his hands for silence.

"Mr. Dracovitch has discovered that Igor's affliction is"—Shane paused for effect—"*love*. He's just been pining away for a girlfriend!"

The place exploded in a roar. Jana laughed so hard she thought her sides would split, and Melanie pounded on Beth's back as she roared.

Clarence Marshall shouted and threw his big yellow ribbon in the air, and it landed in the middle of The Fabulous Five's table right in front of Jana. Still laughing, she took the grubby ribbon between two fingers and threw it back. The next thing she knew the room was filled with flying ribbons as everyone took them off and threw them at Shane and each other.

Mr. Neal passed out ballots at the beginning of homeroom on Wednesday and told them that even though Jana's and Randy's names were the only ones on the ballot for Mr. and Miss Seventh Grade, Mr. Bell thought they should still go through the formalities of voting. He also said that the results would be posted on the bulletin board outside the office during lunch period.

Jana looked at Randy before she made a big X next to his name, and he flashed her his 1,000-watt smile and made a big X near her name. Laura Mc-Call and Melissa McConnell folded up their ballots and stuck them in their notebooks without even voting, and Christie looked back at Jana and gave her a thumbs-up sign.

After lunch, The Fabulous Five hurried to the office to see who the winners were. A large crowd of kids was standing in front of the bulletin board, and it took them a few minutes to be able to work their way close enough to read the list.

"There it is," said Katie, putting her arm around Jana's waist and squeezing her. "You are now officially Miss Seventh Grade of Wacko Junior High."

A tingle ran up and down Jana's spine. "Yes, and Randy is *Mr.* Seventh Grade." While she hadn't wanted to run in the beginning, the thought of Randy and her being elected Mr. and Miss Seventh Grade by all of their friends was so wonderful, she thought she would cry. She was so proud, and she was just as proud of Randy. While she wasn't sure she deserved the honor, there was no doubt in her mind that he did.

"Kaci got Miss Ninth Grade," said Beth.

"Did you actually expect Marsha to beat her?" asked Katie.

"Well, I'm glad to see Chet Miller got Mr. Ninth Grade," said Christie. "He's nice."

"Oh, Garrett Boldt got Mr. Eighth Grade!" squealed Melanie. "I've got to go congratulate him." She quickly squeezed her way out of the crowd.

"It's nice that Shelly Bramlett got Miss Eighth Grade," said Jana. "Although Daphne Alexandrou is super nice, too. I didn't want either one of them to lose."

Suddenly there was shoving, and Jana was pushed aside as Geena McNatt stuck her head in to see the voting results.

"Humph!" she snorted. She glared at Jana, spun around, and pushed her way back out of the crowd.

Jana looked after her. As angry as Geena was, there was a *very* good chance that Jana's plan would work.

That afternoon the feeling was reinforced. As she passed the bulletin board on her way between classes, Jana came to a screeching stop. Her name on the list had been smeared over with a bright red substance. She didn't have to test it to know it was catsup.

CHAPTER

16

"Thanks!" Jana called to Pink as she jumped out of the car and reached into the backseat to take her new dress from the hook. Her stepfather had given her a ride to school so she could keep the dress, which was in a plastic cleaning bag, from getting soiled or wrinkled.

Jana looked around the school yard as she headed toward her friends, who were waiting by the fence. Geena McNatt stopped throwing a football with Clarence Marshall and watched Jana walk by. Jana waved to The Fabulous Five and held the dress high so they could see what she was carrying.

"That is *some gorgeous* dress!" said Beth.

"It's beautiful," said Melanie. "You're going to look *sooo* glamorous in it."

Whitney Larkin and Marcie Bee came over to see it, too, and soon a dozen seventh-grade girls were admiring the dress.

Dekeiska Adams, who hadn't been around when Jana was telling everyone about it before, was asking, "Where in the world did you find such a super dress?"

"At Tanninger's," answered Jana, watching Geena out of the corner of her eye. Geena had dropped the football and walked casually over to where the crowd was gathered.

"When are you going to put it on?" asked Christie. Jana knew that Christie had seen Geena, too.

Speaking loudly so everyone could hear, Jana said, "I'm going to dress in the girls' room by my locker just before I'm supposed to go to the auditorium. I'll keep it in the cleaning bag until then. That way it will stay nice right up until the very last moment."

"We'll meet you at your locker." Katie spoke loudly, too. "But we won't be able to stay with you while you dress. We'll have to go on so we can get good seats. Everyone else will already be in the auditorium."

"That's fine," answered Jana, hoping their conversation didn't seem too planned. "It will only take me a minute or two."

Jana saw Geena going into the building as the first bell rang. Would her plan work? The only alternative if it didn't was to take Geena before the Teen Court, and knowing what Jana did now, she would rather not.

When The Fabulous Five met at Jana's locker, the halls were filled with kids on their way to the auditorium for the awards ceremony. Jana had seen the other winners during the day. Kaci Davis was wearing a beautiful, lacy, burgundy dress, and she had a brand-new perm that made her look terrifically sophisticated. Shelly Bramlett was wearing a slim white dress that looked as if it were made of real silk. Jana had talked to Chet Miller and Garrett Boldt. They had their suits and ties in their locker, as did Randy, and were going to put them on just before the ceremony.

"You'd better hurry," said Christie as they escorted her to the girls' room. "You're not going to have a lot of time."

"I know," said Jana.

"You won't have to worry about it if your plan fails," said Katie. "You won't want to go out onto the stage anyway."

Jana gave her a wry smile. She hoped that wouldn't happen. Her Fabulous Five friends had kept her safe so far. It was all up to her now.

Two eighth-grade girls were leaving as Jana walked into the girls' room, which was empty now.

She hung the dress on the back of a stall door and looked at her watch. She had seven minutes.

Quickly she pulled off her skirt and blouse, folded them, and laid them on the lavatory. Slipping the new dress from the plastic bag, she pulled it on over her head. For a moment, with her head covered up, she felt vulnerable to an attack, and when her head poked through the collar, she looked around quickly to assure herself that no one had slipped into the bathroom.

Jana brushed her hair and put on a little lipstick. There, she thought, looking in the mirror. I'm not as pretty as Kaci Davis, but Randy likes me, and that's what counts.

She hung the clothes she had taken off on the hanger, put it in the plastic bag, and checked her watch again. Twenty seconds to go.

Jana walked to the bathroom door and checked her watch again. Fifteen seconds, ten seconds, five seconds, she counted. Finally she took a deep breath and stepped out.

Mom, Pink, and Mr. McNatt were coming toward her in the hall that led directly to the girls' room. Her mother wore a serious expression, and Pink and Geena's father were smiling. Neither of the men knew about the plan. Mr. McNatt just thought he had been invited because Geena and Jana were going to be friends.

Jana knew she wouldn't be able to see down the intersecting hallways until she had gone about ten feet toward the adults. Now! she thought as she started forward. Nothing happened. Had she been wrong? Just as she had those thoughts, Geena streaked out of the hall on Jana's left. She had the meanest look on her face that Jana had ever seen, and she was pointing the squeeze catsup bottle at Jana with both hands as if it were a gun.

"*You think you're better than everybody!*" she yelled, and squirted a stream of catsup at Jana.

Even though she had been expecting it to happen, Jana was almost too slow in getting out of the way. She dropped her hanging clothes and danced away from the other girl, and the red stream followed her like an arching laser, splattering red on her shoes and ankles. Jana skipped backward and Geena followed her, a vicious smile on her face.

"GEENA!" Mr. McNatt shouted, and ran toward his daughter.

Geena froze, a look of horror on her face.

"WHAT ARE YOU DOING?" He grabbed her by the arm and jerked the catsup bottle away from her.

Jana jumped forward. "NO, MR. MCNATT! Please don't yell at her!"

The big man stared at Jana with a surprised look on his face.

"It's *all right*, Mr. McNatt. She didn't mean it."

"She didn't mean it? How can you say that? She was squirting that stuff at you, wasn't she?"

"Yes, but she doesn't know how to tell someone

she doesn't like them without hitting or doing things like squirting catsup on them."

"She *ought* to know better. She'll have to be punished."

Jana took a deep breath. Was it possible that she could make him listen to her? Or would he shake her off and take Geena home and punish her?

Jana looked right into Mr. McNatt's eyes. "When I ate dinner at your house, I saw Joe and Max punch each other a bunch of times, and," she said, softening her voice, "you hit Max on the hand with a spoon and bumped Joe's and Max's heads together. Geena only knows how to react the ways she's seen at home."

Geena's father's mouth opened as if he were going to say something, but no words came out. Pink looked dumbfounded.

Jana continued quickly before she lost her nerve. "Geena doesn't like me very much, and I kind of understand why now. I guess I *do* have the best of everything. I've got lots of friends that picked me to be Miss Seventh Grade when I didn't even want to be, and my mom has taught me that there are a lot better ways than fighting to solve problems. And," she said, looking shyly at her mother, "she's taught me to be a girl." Her mother's face was beaming with pride.

"Geena doesn't have all those things, and I can't be mad at her for acting the way she does, knowing what I know now."

Geena was looking at Jana with a surprised expression, and Jana thought she felt her father's arm relax.

"Mr. McNatt, I really would like to be Geena's friend. I think she could be a very nice girl." Jana's legs were as limp as ropes when she finished. She didn't know what else to say.

The expression on Mr. McNatt's face changed several times as he looked at Jana. Finally it softened, and he took a deep breath. His voice was calm when he said, "I guess *I'm* the one who didn't understand." He looked at his daughter. "All I know is how to handle men. Tough men. And I don't know how in the world I thought Geena could figure out how to be a girl in a house full of men." His eyes were moist. "Did you mean it when you said you wanted to be her friend?"

"Yes, I do. Very much. But I think Geena should be allowed to pick her own friends. She may not want to be friends with me."

Geena raised her eyes and looked at Jana in surprise.

"Mr. McNatt," said Jana's mother, "I believe my daughter when she says she wants to be friends with your daughter. I believe we should all think about what's happened a little, and then, if they both want to, maybe Geena could go out to lunch with us sometime."

Mr. McNatt reached out and put his arm around his daughter and pulled her close. "I think that's a good idea, Mrs. Pinkerton. And maybe sometime they can go shopping for some girls' things."

Jana was astounded at the look on Geena's face. All the anger that had been in it just minutes before was gone, and her freckled face shone with happiness as she looked up at her father.

Jana shivered with pleasure as she took her mother's hand. Maybe the two of them could help Geena pick out some new clothes.

CHAPTER

17

*J*ana stood where she couldn't be seen in the wings of the stage, waiting for Mr. Bell to finish his speech, which seemed to go on forever. It looked as if The Dreadful Alternatives, who were positioned at the back of the stage, were about to go to sleep. Jana gripped a tissue tightly in each hand to absorb the perspiration from her nervousness. She sneaked a look at Randy. He was watching Mr. Bell and looked as cool as an ice cube. How can he do that? she wondered. Girls were the ones who were supposed to look as if they didn't perspire.

"And now let me introduce to you the president of the seventh-grade class, who will present the winners of *The Wigwam* Mr. and Miss Seventh Grade

109

contest." Mr. Bell turned and held his hand out to indicate Curtis Trowbridge, who came striding out onto the stage as if he had just been elected president of the United States. "Curtis Trowbridge," Mr. Bell finished his introduction.

Curtis adjusted his black horn-rimmed glasses and pulled a sheaf of papers from his suit-coat pocket. Jana was surprised he hadn't rented a tux for the occasion. "Friends! Students! Parents," he began.

Oh, no! Jana couldn't believe it. Curtis was going to make a speech that would probably cover every subject in the encyclopedia.

Kaci Davis threw back her head and closed her eyes in despair, and the other winners shuffled their feet impatiently. Jana noticed bits of tissue sticking out of Kaci's tightly clenched fists, and dark places developing under the arms of her burgundy dress. So, Kaci wasn't as cool as she wanted people to believe, either. The discovery pleased Jana.

After Curtis had been talking for five minutes, some of the kids in the audience started stomping their feet, and Mr. Bell began waving his hands at Curtis and running his finger across his own throat. Curtis finally got the idea and cut his speech off right in the middle of a sentence.

"Uh . . . I guess I'd better introduce our seventh-grade winners now," he said, placing one finger between his eyes and pushing his glasses up. He reached into his pocket and pulled out a three-by-five index card.

Randy leaned close to Jana and whispered, "You'd think this was the Academy Awards."

She smiled and nodded.

"First let me introduce Mr. Congeniality himself," Curtis said with a grand gesture toward the wings where they were standing.

Randy put his hand over his eyes and shook his head in disbelief.

I will *never* be able to get Randy to do anything like this again, thought Jana. And it will be all Curtis Trowbridge's fault.

"RANDY KIRWAN!" Curtis finished his announcement, and The Dreadful Alternatives started playing a rock version of the Wakeman Junior High fight song.

Randy straightened his shoulders and walked out onto the stage as the auditorium was filled with applause, cheers, and whistles.

Tears came to Jana's eyes as she watched him reach out and shake hands with Curtis. Randy looked so handsome.

Jana couldn't remember hearing Curtis announce her name. The applause and cheers rose, and she saw him extending his hand toward her. Randy was smiling a zillion-watt smile at her. She stepped out from the wings, and a roar went up.

When she reached Randy, he beamed down at her

as she curled her arm through his. In the first row, she saw her best friends jumping and cheering with their arms outstretched. Tears ran down her face as she searched the audience for her mom and Pink. They were sitting in the parents section with Mr. McNatt. Geena was sitting next to her father.

Jana put a kiss on her fingertips and blew it to her mother and Pink and smiled at Geena. She thought she saw Geena smile back.

Jana squeezed Randy's arm tight to hold her on the ground.

"Do you think this *really* looks okay on me?" Geena asked Jana. She was standing in front of the mirror wearing a short skirt and matching cotton sweater. True to her mother's word, Mrs. Pinkerton and Jana had invited Geena out for lunch and shopping on Saturday. Jana hadn't been quite sure she was ready to handle Geena so soon, but it was turning out okay.

When they picked her up at her house, Mr. McNatt had come out to the car to talk to them. He had a huge smile on his face and waved as they drove away.

Lunch had been difficult at first. It was hard for Jana to make conversation when all she could think about was yesterday's awards ceremony. It had been everything she could imagine, and her mind kept wandering back to it and that evening when The

Fabulous Five and their friends went to Mama Mia's to have pizza and celebrate.

"I think it looks super on you," Jana answered Geena. "With your color hair that soft green is spectacular. Do you have enough money left from what your father gave you to get a belt for it?"

Geena smiled and nodded.

While Geena fingered through the belt rack, Jana noticed Clarence Marshall and Joel Murphy walking by in the mall. Clarence looked in the store, saw them, and braked to a quick stop, causing Joel to run into him. Clarence tucked in his shirttail and came to the store entrance. Joel scowled at him as he followed.

As Clarence stepped into the store, his eyes were fixed on Geena. He didn't even notice the saleslady who had stepped in front of him. "Can I help you with something?" she asked.

Clarence brushed the hair out of his eyes and said, without looking at where he was pointing, "Um, sure. How much is that?"

"The ladies' lingerie?" asked the lady with surprise in her voice.

A look of horror came over Clarence's face when he saw what he had pointed at. Red crept up from his collar to the tips of his hair, and he stuttered, "Uh, uh, er . . . I think I forgot my money."

Jana laughed so hard her stomach hurt as he scrambled out of the store, with Joel on his heels.

Her mother and Geena, who had not seen Clarence, looked at Jana questioningly. Jana just shook her head and wiped the tears from her eyes. Clarence was a riot.

And then a strange thought occurred to her. Why had he come into the store in the first place? She looked at Geena. Clarence had been hanging around Geena a lot lately. Could it be possible that he liked her? The idea boggled Jana's mind. Clarence liked Geena? She looked at Geena. Stranger things have happened, I guess, she thought, closing her mouth, which had dropped open in astonishment. She smiled to herself and walked over to help Geena pick out a belt.

CHAPTER

18

"Who do you think you are?"

Melanie Edwards blinked to attention and looked at Mrs. Clark, her Family Living teacher, who was asking the question of the class.

The students glanced around at each other and shrugged.

Mrs. Clark smiled and went on, "You are a child to your parents, a student to your teachers, a library card number, a locker number, a statistic in the population figures of this town. And if you play sports, you have a number on your shirt. But who *are* you?"

What is she getting at? thought Melanie. I know who I am. I'm Melanie Edwards, and I'm in seventh grade at Wakeman Junior High. I have a mother and a father, a little brother, and three gorgeous boy-friends, Scott Daly, Shane Arrington, and Garrett Boldt. Well, maybe they aren't all three *exactly* boy-friends, but . . .

Mrs. Clark was speaking again. "Have you ever wondered what makes you different from your best friend? From everyone you know? From everybody else on earth? Your looks are different. You think differently. You have your own interests and hob-bies. You like some things and hate others. You are special. *Unique*. Aren't you?"

This time everyone was nodding and smiling to each other. Melanie caught Jana's eye and grinned broadly. Even the members of The Fabulous Five were all different from each other. But that was okay. They were still best friends.

Mrs. Clark's voice broke into her thoughts again. "How would you like to start a special class project that will let each one of you find out exactly who you are and why you're special?"

Cheers broke out all over the room, and it took Mrs. Clark several minutes to quiet everyone down. Melanie was excited, too. It would be fun to find out what made her special and maybe even find out things about other people, too. For instance, what made Laura McCall so snooty? And Shane Ar-rington so cool and laid-back? And even why she and Katie had such opposite opinions about boys?

*   *   *

What *will* Melanie find out about herself and others? Read the surprising answers in *The Fabulous Five #15: Melanie's Identity Crisis.*

ABOUT THE AUTHOR

Betsy Haynes, the daughter of a former newswoman, began scribbling poetry and short stories as soon as she learned to write. A serious writing career, however, had to wait until after her marriage and the arrival of her two children. But that early practice must have paid off, for within three months Mrs. Haynes had sold her first story. In addition to a number of magazine short stories and the Taffy Sinclair series, Mrs. Haynes is also the author of *The Great Mom Swap* and its sequel, *The Great Boyfriend Trap*. She lives in Colleyville, Texas, with her husband, who is also an author.